DIRTY GAME

DIRTY MAFIA GAMES

MIKA LANE

HEADLANDS PUBLISHING

COPYRIGHT

Copyright© 2019 by Mika Lane
Headlands Publishing
4200 Park Blvd. #244
Oakland, CA 94602

BE THE FIRST TO KNOW...

Want more heat, heart,
and bad boys who know what they're doing?
Join my list and I'll send the steam straight to your inbox,
starting with a deliciously naughty story:

SIGN UP TO MY MAILING LIST!
Or visit:
https://geni.us/free-book-signup

1

LUCA

Why had I let my brother drag me to Loaded Dice again? Yeah, we had business to attend to, but I fucking hated the place.

It was a shitty strip club in a shitty part of Las Vegas with a suck-up jerk of an owner and the most second- and third-rate strippers you'd ever seen.

Seriously. This was where old strippers went to die.

Yeah, that's a dick thing to say, but hell if it wasn't true. Dudes hung out here because the drinks were cheap and the free buffet was always stocked. And I supposed, after a few bourbons, the girls started looking a little better.

Shit, you could come here, spend five dollars on a beer, stuff your belly with fried food, and be on your way. For some guys, a homely naked girl was better than no naked girl at all.

And the place was nearly always packed.

But now, at nine a.m.-ish, when people in Las Vegas were either finally going to bed for the night or just getting up, there was a lull, which I'm sure was welcome by the folks that kept Loaded Dice running around the clock.

Such was life in Sin City. And it had been my life, well—all my life.

Leo and I had some shit to take care of there, so I was sucking up the second-rated-ness of the place for as long as I had to. Nothing trumped business.

Not the time of day or night.

Not shitty strippers.

Not bad food or cheap beer.

Nope, none of that.

I glanced at Leo—my twin brother, closest friend, and worst enemy—as he watched the lone dancer up on stage. The sarcastic half-smile on his face gave nothing away. He didn't wear that expression because he was watching a bored-as-shit gyrating woman who'd rather be at home with her kids. No, he'd be wearing the same smirk if he'd just met Angelina Jolie and she knelt down to suck his dick.

He called it his poker face. I called it his *resting bitch face*.

I turned to him. "Yo. That one gonna be your little

missus? I can see it now, all of you around the Thanksgiving table…"

He kept his eyes on the dancer. "Fuck off."

At least he was in a good mood.

I was the older of the two of us by five minutes. And like most elder children, I was the one who had my shit together.

Well, as together as anyone affiliated with 'organized crime' can be

Leo, on the other hand, was the typical impetuous younger sibling, prone to bad tempers, vengeance, and fucking anything with two legs and a pussy.

Actually, the two legs thing was optional.

But between us, we made a pretty good team.

Not that we had any choice.

On our fourteenth birthdays, our Pop had sat us down.

"Boys, you are old enough now to become part of the family business."

I remembered this clear as day.

Leo and I looked at each other excitedly. Even though we lived in an affluent section of Las Vegas, we loved that our dad's businesses were in the rough parts of town, dealing with and making money off the poor bastards who were down on their luck, couldn't seem to get a break, or were just too fucked up to make a smart goddamn good decision.

Dad owned pawnshops and liquor stores. Pretty much every teenage boy's idea of nirvana. All the booze we wanted and tons of cool shit to fuck with in his shops.

And he was going to give us jobs there! We'd be the envy of everybody in our private school.

Actually, we already were. *The Borroni twins*, as we were known. Massively popular for some reason that was beyond me, we were also the smartest kids in school and known for the kick-ass parties our parents would let us throw in our basement rec room.

Lots of making out and finger fucking in the closets and dark corners, and so much alcohol that by the time I was sixteen, I decided I never wanted another drink in my life.

Hadn't had a drink since.

But Pop didn't so much as give us jobs as indoctrinate us into a life we'd suspected was his, which we'd never been entirely sure how to define before then.

And this life—also known as *the business*—was something we were preordained to join him in. It didn't matter if we'd hoped to do something else with our lives. We were joining *the family* and were warned that if we didn't, it would mean grave things for our loved ones. Not only livelihoods would be in danger, but also *lives*.

There was no looking back.

Heavy shit for a fourteen-year-old, but hey, it had been like that for generations. And it would be like that for us, too.

Over time, we learned that Pop's liquor stores and

pawnshops were fronts for laundering the huge amounts of cash that passed through the casinos and other businesses he and his 'brothers' had their fingers in. It was complex, it was dangerous, and it was exciting as hell.

And it wasn't without its downsides.

2

LUCA

THE BORED STRIPPER who'd captivated my brother had left the stage, replaced by someone younger and more eager. That was how they all started out—a little shy, maybe even embarrassed, but hoping to make enough money to send some back home or save for a rainy day. If they got out when they were young enough, the cash could be a good head start on a life that would otherwise be unattainable.

I had some admiration for the women who got up on that stage, or any stage, anywhere. They were doing what they had to and making horny dudes happy at the same time. It was a win-win.

But regardless, I wouldn't let anyone I loved take a job like that. Fuck no.

Guess I was a goddamn hypocrite. There I was,

watching the strippers, but I wouldn't let my worst enemy become one. How fucked was that?

Leo leaned toward me so I could hear him over the blaring house music. Exactly what you wanted to jam to at nine thirty in the morning.

"Be right back," he said, getting up and tucking in his already perfectly-tucked in shirt.

"Don't be long. You know we have shit to do," I said.

He gave me the smirk. "I just wanna say hi to a friend backstage." He wandered off, with the proprietor's hawk eye following him closely.

Most patrons in Loaded Dice were not allowed anywhere near the backstage area. But Bob wanted to stay on our good side and let us do whatever we wanted.

In fact, he once told me Leo had fucked a girl right on his desk.

"Here you go, Mr. Borroni."

Ah, Echo. The only bright light in the shithole that was this dive had just delivered my soda water.

I looked up at the object of my affection, the beautiful Echo, whose pale skin and black hair spun me inside out every fucking time I saw her.

What was it with this woman?

Yeah, she had a killer body with her curvy ass, perky tits, and tiny waist. The waitress costume she wore—a red satin bustier and short, swingy skirt—looked like it'd been made for her.

"You don't have to call me Mr. Borroni, Echo. Call me Luca."

She smiled and laughed, glancing at Bob, whom I'd seen scold her for talking too much to patrons.

But he'd probably let her bullshit with me all day long if I wanted her to. That's how fawning he was.

We had an interesting… relationship.

I gestured toward her boss, who was heading our way. "Don't worry, Echo, you won't get in trouble."

"Well, I don't know about that. I was a bit late this morning, so I'm already in the dog house," she laughed nervously.

She scooted over to another table, full of what looked like guys in town for some sort of tech convention.

Probably patting themselves on the back for slumming it.

I could hear it now.

Dude, you should have seen the shithole we checked out off the Strip! It was classic old Vegas. And fucking cheap, too!

If they gave Echo any shit, I'd make sure they were sorry they'd ventured over to this part of town. They'd never leave the safety of the Bellagio or Aria again.

All the swinging dicks that came to this town thinking they could shit and piss all over us and leave the mess behind irritated me to no end.

But lucky for them, they were polite to Echo, probably seeing in her the same thing I did. She had a quiet dignity about her and treated customers respectfully, as well.

I suppose it was a protective thing, but I'd seen plenty of cocktail waitresses—who, god knew, had to put up with no end of male bullshit—mock their customers, treating them with nothing better than vicious disdain.

One on hand, I couldn't blame them. These women got their asses squeezed all day long by drunk frat boys and conventioneers who hadn't gotten out of their Podunk towns in so long, they didn't know how to think without their 'old lady' bossing them around. These were the guys who were too stupid to wrap their dicks when they spent an hour fucking an escort and ended up bringing home no end of health problems that revealed their infidelity.

Dumbasses.

But Echo was kind and patient, treating everyone the same—making customers feel important and welcome, and shutting down any wandering hands with a firm calm that gained the respect of even the most drunk asshole.

Yeah, I'd been watching her a lot since I'd been coming to the club for business stuff. Might as well make the best of it.

She hadn't been at Loaded Dice for long—maybe a couple weeks. But she'd caught my eye her first day, working her ass off and helping her fellow waitresses.

I'd tried to chat her up, but she was private as hell,

at least at work. I could relate, though, because I was pretty much the same way.

And I had to say I dug a woman who didn't dump her life story on me in the first five minutes I'd met her.

I guess her quiet self-respect reminded me a little of myself. Like she could see the forest through the trees —kept her eye on the ball—or whatever goddamn corny cliché matched the situation. I wanted to know more about her, and I had a plan to make just that happen.

Actually, I had a plan to make a lot of shit happen with the lovely Echo.

3

LUCA

Bob sidled over to our table. "Where'd your brother go, Luca?"

I craned my neck toward the stage, where the young lady dancing had stopped to collect a scattering of dollar bills from the edge of the stage, stuffing them in her little rhinestone-encrusted purse.

"I think he went to say hi to someone."

Bob hooked his thumbs in the pockets of his polyester pants. "Hey, I've got great seats to the upcoming UNLV basketball game."

I felt kind of bad about the disdain I held for Bob. I mean, he wasn't a horrible person—nothing like that. He was just kind of douchey and wasn't always on the up-and-up with business people around town.

Like the guy who ran my organization.

Sal Matteo. One person you didn't want to piss off.

But Bob had pissed Sal off to the point of no return. Bob, basically, was screwed.

And this was the day of his reckoning.

He just didn't know it yet.

"Thanks, man. I'm not much of a fan, but I appreciate the invite," I said.

His face fell. "Oh. Okay. Well, maybe Leo will want to come."

Leo? Fuck no.

"Oh yeah, ask him. He's a huge fan."

I loved setting my brother up.

Time to get the ball rolling. "Hey, Bob, do you mind if I have your lovely Echo run a little errand for me?"

A smile lit up his face. "No. Not at all."

Idiot didn't even know what I was going to ask for, but he loaned her out nonetheless.

I waved Echo over and pressed a hundred-dollar bill in her hand to run down the block to the sub shop for me.

Like I was going to eat a sub at nine forty-five a.m.

She grabbed her jacket from behind the bar and took off. In the seconds the club's front door was open, the blinding morning light flashed in and over the interior, highlighting the dirt and grime that never got cleaned in a place that never closed.

Leo was heading back over to me wearing his usual expression, when someone tapped my shoulder.

"Hello," I said.

"Um, hi," a nervous young guy said, pushing his hands deep into his pockets. "I was wondering if you could give me a job?"

Gutsy. I liked that.

Unfortunately, that's not how we expanded our empire.

I stood while waiting for Leo. "Why don't you give me your number? I'll call you if we have anything."

The kid reached for a napkin and using the pen I'd handed him, scribbled down something illegible.

"Thanks, man," he said, sounding hopeful.

I turned my back to him so he'd know our conversation was over.

"Got everything taken care of? The girls all gone?"

Leo nodded. "Yeah, man. They split. We're good to go. No more coming back here."

What a fucking relief.

I waved at several of my associates, who'd made themselves at home in the dingy corners of the club. They emerged from the dark, and pulled their weapons out.

Shots rang out all around us, and within moments, Leo and I were the only people left standing, aside from my hit men. Their job finished, they took off out the back door as soon as I gave them the nod, while my brother and I surveyed the damage, both collateral and otherwise.

When news of this got out, it would keep the white bread frat boys out of this part of town for a while.

4

ECHO

I REMEMBER when I thought a hundred dollars was all the money in the world.

It wasn't that long ago, really.

And there I was, admiring the beauty of a crisp hundred in my hand, smooth with that powdery texture fresh bills had. I stuffed the 'Benjamin'—that's what people around here called a hundred dollar bill—deep in my pocket before anyone on the street spotted it in my possession, and tugged on the hem of my windbreaker to cover my short skirt.

My *very* short skirt.

Just because I was a cocktail waitress, where I wore skirts so short the cheeks of my ass dipped in and out of view, didn't mean I wanted everyone on the street to see my goods.

No, those were reserved for the paying customers of Loaded Dice, one of Las Vegas's seedier strip joints.

Like many places in Vegas, Loaded Dice was open around the clock. Once inside the joint, thanks to the dim lighting and absence of windows, you'd never know what time of day it was. Which was the whole idea.

You could party twenty-four seven and never be distracted by the annoying thought that maybe you shouldn't be doing tequila shots at eight in the morning.

Las Vegas was designed to keep people unbothered by the propriety that ruled their lives elsewhere. It's why people visited. Rules, responsibilities, and even respectability were left at home, or if not at home, at least in the suitcase in your room. And what happened in Vegas—well, everyone knew how *that* saying went.

When I'd first come to Vegas, I'd gotten a job at a shitty little pawnshop. Christ, the stories I could tell about that place—the down-and-out folks who came in, desperate to sell whatever they owned for some quick cash, usually to be gambled away in the casinos and then lost as fast as they got it.

Lucky for me, the folks who owned the pawnshop also owned Loaded Dice, and after I proved myself a reliable employee, they let me move over there, where I hoped to make some big-ass tips. So far, so good. I'd only been there a couple weeks, but it seemed like a lucrative gig.

But two weeks was long enough to get to know some of the club's regulars, like the twin brothers Luca and Leo Borroni. I didn't know a damn thing about them except they seemed to stop by almost daily, and they were so fucking good-looking that when they walked in, everyone—women *and* men—stopped what they were doing to watch them walk by.

I had no idea what they did for work, but in a place like Vegas, you don't ask a lot of questions, especially when someone's a good tipper. I learned that early on. You just wait on them with a smile and remember to always say *thank you*.

"Well, if it isn't the lovely Echo," Luca had said that morning when I served his club soda and his brother's scotch.

Funny that identical twins drank such different beverages. I mean, there would have been no telling the two guys apart if Luca didn't have facial hair and Leo wasn't completely clean-shaven.

Otherwise, they were exactly the same. Glittering hazel eyes, heavy brows, and strong, masculine jaws. Their thick black hair brushed back in a way that indicated they made some effort, but also that they didn't try too hard.

The very definition of manliness, if you asked me.

But what did I know? I just brought the guys their drinks and offered polite small talk.

5

ECHO

"Here you go, Mr. Borroni," I said, waiting for him to insist I call him Luca, like he always did.

I'd almost said *good morning*, which was a big no-no. We weren't supposed to remind people they were drinking in a strip club at an hour that in the real world might not be considered appropriate.

The only actual indication that it might be morning was that we were between shifts—the all-night gals had gone home, and the day shift strippers were starting to trickle in.

I'd been playing around with the idea of becoming a stripper, myself. Not that I wanted to get naked and shake my ass in five-inch heels, but damn if those ladies didn't make *bank*. The ones who really busted ass and took every extra shift they could get their hands on made well over a couple hundred grand a year.

A few years of earnings like that and a person could sit back and decide what they *really* wanted to do with their life.

And I wanted to do a lot.

As Luca made small talk and I tried to respond politely without being distracted by the way his gaze bored into mine, I glanced around for my boss, Bob. He was pissed I'd come in late because he'd had to serve drinks for the few minutes he was waiting on me. I was reliable most of the time, which was more than he could say for a lot of the other cocktail waitresses he had on staff.

But I didn't want to push my luck and annoy him any further by bullshitting with a customer when I was supposed to be serving half the club. People spent a lot of money on booze at Loaded Dice, which was important to Bob. Actually, it was important to me too, because the more they spent on booze, the more tips I earned.

And I had plans for my money. Big plans.

And don't you know, Bob was headed over my way, where I was trapped in conversation with the gorgeous Luca. I had to take deep breaths to keep from babbling like an idiot, that's how nervous his staring made me.

Not so much with his brother Leo, who, as the quieter one, was scanning the club like he was looking for someone. Probably waiting for his favorite girl to come onstage.

Bob extended Luca his hand with a giant grin, like he was greeting long-lost friends.

"The Borroni brothers. I'm so honored to have you in my establishment."

I never did understand Bob's obsequiousness. The guys came in all the time from what I could see.

"Bob, good to see you," Luca said, returning the handshake.

Leo just nodded.

Luca put his hand on Bob's arm and gestured toward me with his chin. "Hey, can I borrow your lovely girl here, for a few minutes? I need her to run a quick errand for me."

What? I wasn't a damn errand girl.

But Bob couldn't have looked more thrilled to loan me out.

I was *not* thrilled. I was busy trying to earn some tips, for heaven's sake.

But, of course, I said none of that. I just smiled, like I always did.

Luca reached inside his breast pocket, retrieving his wallet, and rifled through a stack of bills. He pulled one out and handed it to me.

A hundred-dollar bill. A *Benjamin.*

He pressed it into my palm. "Echo, would you go to the shop down the block and pick up a meatball sub for me? Be sure to have them add swiss. And keep the change."

I held the bill between my thumb and forefinger and turned to Bob, waiting for him to say he needed me at the club and ask why the guy didn't go buy his own meatball sub, for Christ's sake.

But Bob did not say that.

Nor did he ask who the hell eats a meatball sub for breakfast.

"Sure, Luca, no problem." He turned to me. "Echo, I'll cover for you while you're gone. Go on, now."

I must have looked at him like he'd gone insane because he patted me on the back and walked me in the direction of the door.

I grabbed my windbreaker from behind the bar, and when we were out of earshot, I leaned toward him. "You sure this is okay? I mean, it seems kind of weird."

He looked over at the twins and waved at them, smiling.

I could have sworn he was nervous.

"Totally fine, Echo. They're good... customers. I want to keep them happy. And hey, you got a pretty big tip out of it, didn't you?"

I shrugged. "As long as you're okay with it. Hey, while I have you, I wanted to ask if I could work Thanksgiving. The girls say it's super busy then."

He rolled his eyes. "Yes, yes. Now please get going. The man asked for a sub, I'm guessing because he's hungry. Let's not keep him waiting."

6

ECHO

WHEN I STEPPED OUTSIDE of Loaded Dice, *Benjamin* in hand, the bright Vegas sun, in contrast to the dark club interior, hit me like a slap across the face. I squinted while my eyes adjusted, and my ears filled with the sounds of the morning rush—also a jarring contrast to the club's booming house music. The strong desert breeze whipped hair around my face, and while I'd only been indoors for an hour or so, the change in scenery was kind of refreshing.

I trudged over to the sub shop, well aware that my ass was hanging out, and placed Luca's order. Because I had a few minutes to kill, I got myself a vanilla shake and dialed my sister in West Virginia.

"Dini. How are ya?" I asked when she picked up.

"Echo, hi. I'm *great*. How about you?"

My sweet, sweet little sister. Younger by three years and nicer than me by any measure.

I knew my sister, and when she said she was doing *great*, I knew she wasn't.

Dini was never great. Life had handed her the shit end of the stick, and while she tried to make the best of things—her life in a wheelchair and dependency on our messed-up mother—there was only so much fake happiness she could pull off.

"What's going on? Where is Mom?" I asked.

Rhetorical questions. We knew where Mom was. In a general sense, anyway.

I could hear Dini wheeling around the house. "She's not here, Echo. I haven't seen her in a couple days."

Off on a bender, no doubt. Which would be fucking fine if she didn't have a wheelchair-bound daughter at home who depended on her for food and shelter.

I took a deep breath as the sub shop guy called my name and handed me a white bag. "Dini, do you have any food? I know how she left you last time—"

"There's not much, Echo. But I was going to call the neighbor."

"Fucking hell," I said. "I'm calling the grocery store and having food delivered to you. Dini, when this shit happens, you have to *let me know*."

We'd had this conversation before, and the fact was that Dini would never ask me for a thing. That's why I had to check in with her all the time.

She was silent for a moment. "Thank you, Echo. I

appreciate it. There are a few things in the house. I was about to make some oatmeal."

For fuck's sake.

"Dini—"

But she interrupted me because there really wasn't anything to say that hadn't already been said. Many times.

Our mom was a fuckup, and I'd left Dini behind to deal with it, something that ate at me day and night. So, I tried to do what I could from the other side of the country.

"Echo, don't. Don't go there. We both know it is what it is. We just gotta deal with it. There's no choice," she said.

I'd been begging her to come to Vegas and live with Yasmina and me since the minute I'd arrived. She always had one excuse or another, but I wasn't giving up.

I sighed. "I'll order you some groceries. But you know, you can too—just use the credit card I gave you."

"Oh. About the credit card. Mom found it. She took it. I meant to call you. You might want to cancel it."

Was she fucking kidding? How many times had I told her to keep that card out of our mother's reach?

"Okay, Dini. I'll send you some money, too, but keep it out of Mom's sight. You know she'll just take it and spend it. In fact, some guy at the club just gave me a hundred bucks to get him a sub and told me to keep the change."

She laughed, which was music to my ears. Dini didn't laugh very often. "Oh my god, you have some serious weirdos out there."

"Yup, we do. Las Vegas is an interesting place."

"Love you, big sis."

Damn if my throat didn't catch. I had to get Dini out of my mother's clutches, and out west where I could look after her and make sure that in spite of her chair, she could thrive like anybody else.

She was such a good kid—she deserved no less.

"Bye, Dini. Call me next time you need anything, okay?"

"Yes, ma'am," she said.

I grabbed Luca's sub and took a long draw on my shake as I meandered back to Loaded Dice. I didn't want to be a pain in the ass by taking my sweet time, but it was awesome to be out in the fresh air.

I stepped it up. There was money to be made, seedy strip club or not.

7

ECHO

I PULLED open Loaded Dice's heavy door, waiting a sec for my eyes to adjust from the blinding morning sun to the club's dim interior.

As I tried to look around, temporarily blinded, I noticed a strange smell. It wasn't the usual slightly stale beer odor I'd learned to ignore. No, it was as if someone had burned something in the kitchen. Had one of the cooks gotten drunk again? Just the other day one of them had forgotten a basket of fries in the cooking oil. The smell was so bad, we almost had to close.

Almost.

Loaded Dice offered the same shitty bar food every other place in Vegas did, and our customers scarfed it up like they were starving prisoners. Unfortunately, the short-order cooks drank as much as our patrons, which was a dangerous combination.

But this didn't smell like a kitchen disaster.

It was more chemical-y, like the fireworks on the Fourth of July that had been so popular in the small town I'd grown up in.

But no one would light fireworks *inside*, would they?

That would just be crazy.

As my vision adjusted, I glanced through the dark for Bob. The door swung shut behind me, and as I stepped, something blocked my foot. I took another step, and my feet were no longer under me. I went flying forward.

I watched as the bag of food I'd gotten for Luca, as well as my vanilla milkshake, launched from my grip in slow motion. I barely got my hands under me before my face smashed into the smelly, carpeted floor.

The weird thing was that I'd tripped over something large and soft.

Had someone left a bag of garbage in front of the front door? Who the hell would do that? We had a dumpster out back.

The club was eerily silent. I mean, the house music was still *bam-bam-bamming*, but there was no movement.

No people.

Something was off. Very off.

And for Christ's sake, I'd only been gone ten minutes, tops.

I looked at the source of my fall, and in the dim light, crawled closer to confirm that it was *not*, actually, a bag of garbage.

No, it was a man, crumpled as if he'd just fallen where he stood. And in his stillness and awkward position, I was pretty sure he was no longer alive.

Holyfuckingshit.

I'd stumbled over a *body*. A body, as in, a *no longer alive human being*. Right there, in the doorway of Loaded Dice, where I'd been serving drinks just a few minutes before.

I scrambled up by pushing against it, the scream building in my throat choked off by abject terror. As I struggled to get my feet back under me, I got something red and sticky all over my hands. While I wiped them down the front of my windbreaker, I glanced around, my eyes now pretty well adjusted to the dark.

The body I'd fallen over?

It wasn't the only one.

Nope.

Random dead were scattered around like cockroaches after an extermination. And that included Bob, who was slumped over the bar.

Someone had killed Bob?

Ohmygod.

Was that smell… from guns?

With a shriek, I turned to run back out the door.

Unfortunately, I stepped right into my spilled shake. I wiped out again. Now I was *really* covered in sticky goo.

At least I didn't fall on the body again.

While I was trying to get my feet under me, someone called my name.

"*Echo.* Wait."

CHAPTER 8

ECHO

WHO THE FUCK WAS THAT? Someone was alive?

I turned to see Luca Borroni coming toward me with long strides.

Why was he alive when everyone else was dead?

Finding my voice, I screeched, leaping over the body that had initially tripped me. I was pushing the club's door open to escape, when Luca caught up to me and gripped my arm so hard I knew I'd have a bruise later.

"Let me go!" I shrieked, trying to shake him off me.

I had to get out. I pounded him with my free hand, and when that didn't get me free, I went for his face.

But he held me at arm's length, where I couldn't do any damage.

"Echo, calm down for fuck's sake. Please calm down," he said, pulling me back inside the club.

My legs buckled in fear, leaving me on top of the dead body again.

"No, no, no, Luca. Please don't kill me. You can't. I take care of my little sister. She's in a wheelchair. Please, I'll do anything."

He yanked me up to my feet with his death grip and grabbed my chin with his free hand, turning me to him.

"I. Said. Calm. Down."

I closed my eyes. My life was over. What the fuck would Dini do? I couldn't count on my mom to take care of her. She was an unreliable mess.

Why was this happening?

Then the tears came.

"No, no, no," I wailed, still struggling to get out of his grip.

Had he killed all these people? And was it now my turn?

He gripped my chin tighter and shook me, getting so close I could feel his breath.

"Echo, look at me," he growled.

I forced my eyes to open. Luca was going to be the last person I saw before I died.

"I'm getting you out of here. No one's killing you," he said.

"Oh please, Luca, don't hurt me," I blubbered.

"No one is going to hurt you. You are safe." He gripped my hand and with one glance at the carnage behind him, pulled me out the door. "Come with me. C'mon."

I didn't really have any choice but to follow him. The grip he had on my hand tightened, and he was moving so fast I had to jog to keep up. I looked down to see my windbreaker covered in blood and vanilla shake, and in the confusion I'd lost one shoe, my pantyhose quickly shredding on my bare foot.

Luca looked down to see what was holding me up. "Lose the shoe. C'mon."

In no condition to argue, I shook my one remaining high heel off and thrust it into the gutter. Barefoot didn't feel good on my tender feet, but at least I could keep up.

"Where are we going?" I cried.

We stopped at a huge Toyota pickup truck. He pressed a button and helped me up into the passenger seat.

When he'd gotten in on the driver side, I had half a mind to jump out and run. But he reached for my hands. Both of them.

He leaned toward me, speaking in a slow, even voice. "Echo, you need to calm down. Take some deep breaths."

I took a deep breath. It didn't help.

"Wh… what happened back there? Did you d… do that?" In my heart I knew the answer, but I had to ask. And I had a feeling that calling the police was out of the question.

"I did not. But I know who did. It was a hit."

A *hit*? What the hell was a *hit*?

"What happened to all the people I worked with? What about the girls?"

"The girls got out. Leo warned them. Just like I sent you out to keep you safe."

Realization didn't just wash over me, it hit me like a closed fist. The little breakfast I'd had a few hours earlier, and my recent shake, decided they no longer wanted to be in my stomach.

Apparently, *queasy* was written all over my face.

"Open the door if you're getting sick."

When I didn't move, Luca reached across me and pushed the door open. I leaned out just in time to avoid making a disgusting mess of his truck.

After I got sick, I gradually eased myself back in, sputtering and coughing, and he reached across me to pull the door closed. He fastened my seat belt for me and began to drive.

He handed me a bottle of water. "Here. Drink some of this."

The bottle was still sealed, thank god. I about to consume anything this man might have tampered with.

"Just a couple sips, okay? Take it slow. Hey, do you want a Xanax? Might help you calm down."

I turned to him. "You have Xanax? Why would you have Xanax?"

He shrugged as he turned into traffic and accelerated.

Did everybody carry Xanax except for me?

"Where are we going?" I asked.

Now that I was past hysteria, the adrenaline was kicking in. I sank down, really far down, in my seat. If Luca was not the killer, whoever it was could be close by. My life might be about to end, but I sure as hell wasn't going to be a damn sitting duck.

"So all the dancers are okay?"

He nodded. "Yup. At least as far as I know."

"What's that mean, *at least as far as you know*? Are you fucking kidding me? You survived the shooting and didn't look around to see who else might have?" I shrieked.

"Echo, your boss Bob owed some people a lot of money. Some might even say he stole from them."

Was he serious? Bob owed someone money and now he was dead?

"What the fuck. Someone shot him just 'cause he owed them money? Why didn't they let him pay it back?" I fished my phone out of my windbreaker pocket. "I'm calling the cops."

But before I could even enter my passcode, Luca had swiped the phone out of my hand and slipped it into his back pocket.

"Okay. We need to have a talk." He pulled over into a residential area.

CHAPTER 9

ECHO

THAT WAS IT. I was done for. I could see it now.

Cocktail waitress murdered and dumped in nice Las Vegas suburb… killer at large.

Yup. That was going to be my story. My legacy.

He reached for my soiled windbreaker, but I smacked his hand away.

"Don't you touch me!"

I reached for the door handle, but he must have pressed some button or child safety lock because, just like in the movies, the door wouldn't open for me.

Because of course.

But I did follow his gaze. I was filthy and disgusting, and my pantyhose were no more than a few threads of nylon trying to hang onto my legs. I felt in my pockets, where I found my wallet, keys, a lipstick, and the change from money he'd given me earlier. That was small comfort.

"Listen to me, please," he said in a calm voice. "Bob was doing business with some scary men. He crossed them, and he paid the price. He knew he had it coming, that's why he always tried to be so nice to me. But I couldn't do anything to save him."

"So somebody killed him and everyone else in the club? Is that how things are handled? That's *murder*."

He looked straight ahead and said nothing. "The important thing is that you are safe. Now, we need to get you cleaned up."

I shook my head. "No. Just take me home."

He looked puzzled. "You can't go home."

"*What?*"

"It's not safe for you there. At least not right now."

Fuck.

"But I have a roommate. Is she safe?"

He nodded. "Yes, she'll be fine. I saw to it that nothing would happen to her, either."

Okay, now I was completely confused. But I decided to focus on one thing at a time.

"How am I going to get cleaned up when I can't go to my own home to shower and put on fresh clothes? Are you going to give me something to wear?"

He reached into the pickup truck's backseat and produced a long, tan trench coat and a pair of white Pumas. "Put these on. We'll go to one of my shops where you can get some new clothes."

"You have shops?"

He started driving again. "My brother and I have all sorts of businesses."

He pressed a button on his steering wheel, which must have dialed somebody.

"Hi, Sylvia. Hey, I'll be in with someone in ten minutes or so. We'll come up the back elevator, okay? Can you have some things ready for a size—"

He looked over at me. "What size are you?" he asked.

"Ten. I am a size ten."

He nodded. "Did you hear that Sylvia? We need some clothes in size ten."

Her response came back tinny and broken. "Okay, boss. We'll be ready for you," was all I could make out.

My head was spinning. Nothing made sense. I was cocktailing at my new job, ran an errand for a customer, and returned to find my boss and everyone else in the place dead.

And now, the guy who I was pretty sure was responsible for it all was *taking me fucking shopping*?

Was this a joke?

Because it sure felt like one.

You know, like that old-school show, *Candid Camera*. Or the newer-old show, *Punk'd*.

Except none of it felt very funny. Not at all.

And as if all that wasn't fucked enough, an hour later, I was clean and dressed head to toe in new duds from Luca's fancy store.

They'd even gotten me new undies and a matching bra. I'd never had a matching set before.

His employee, Sylvia, had whisked me away as soon as I'd gotten off some sort of private elevator to a fancy bathroom where I could clean up. Then, she wheeled in a hanging rack of clothes for me to choose from.

And she stood there, watching.

"You can have all of them. Just pick something for right now," she said.

Um, what?

She smiled kindly. "Want me to pick for you?"

I nodded mutely and continued to just stand there wrapped in a white towel.

Sylvia helped me into my new panties and bra, and then pulled a pair of skinny jeans up my hips, and a lightweight sweater with bell sleeves over my head. She showed me to a little chair and proceeded to pull socks over my feet and then zipped some high-heeled booties onto them.

She handed me a little clutch bag. "Put your phone and things in here. All your clothes are being thrown away."

I dropped my waitressing uniform and windbreaker into a large garbage bag that she held open.

Just as I finished, Luca appeared. Sylvia conveniently made herself scarce.

"Wow. Look at you," he said, his eyes traveling over me from head to toe.

Shit.

I was afraid of him. To be honest, I hated him a little, too.

But his gaze made my heart jump, dammit, in spite of my need for self-preservation. I squeezed my thighs together to quell the feeling that was starting to betray me.

"Thank you," I said, gesturing to my clothing.

"You're welcome. Now, let's go to lunch."

CHAPTER 10

ECHO

Just like that? Go to lunch? Kill people, take a girl shopping, and go to fucking lunch?

What show was I in now? *Twilight Zone?*

"Really? I'm not sure I'm hungry."

It hadn't exactly been one of the best days of my life.

He just stared at me.

"Okay, okay, I'll go," I said, walking to the elevator, new clutch in hand.

Fifteen minutes later we were seated in a tucked away booth at the Eiffel Tower restaurant in the Paris hotel.

Un-fucking-believable.

The waiter popped by as soon as we were seated. "Wonderful to see you, Mr. Borroni. What can I get for you and your guest?"

"The usual, thanks."

What the fuck was 'the usual'?

And how did he know whether or not I wanted some?

But before I could think about it much more, a dozen oysters were brought to the table, along with bottle of champagne. A glass was poured for me and a Perrier for Luca.

"I'm starving," he said, diving in.

Murder will do that to you, I suppose.

Myself, not so much. I took a little sip of from the water glass the waiter had just set in front of me.

"Luca, what happened to your brother, Leo? Is he… okay?" I had to ask.

Luca slurped an oyster he'd dipped in some watery-looking stuff. "He's fine. He left before I did."

Oh. So organized.

"Don't you like oysters?" he asked.

"I've never had one. Not sure I'm in the mood right now to try one."

He picked up a half-shell, spooned some cocktail sauce on top of it, and directed it toward my lips. "C'mon. Open up."

Oh, what the hell.

Luca proceeded to introduce me to the delicate art of enjoying oysters. They weren't all that bad. A little salty and slimy, but I could stomach one or two.

"So, Echo, there is something I wanted to discuss with you."

God, he was handsome. I hated that about him.

And it was so unfair the universe made *two* of him, essentially.

"What's that?"

"Since I saved you—"

I leaned toward him. "Excuse me? *Saved* me? You did no such thing."

He leaned back slightly in his chair and looked at me. I could swear I saw amusement on his face.

I wouldn't have minded smacking it right off, too.

"I could have run out of there. I didn't need you to save me," I said, sitting back in my chair.

So there.

"Oh, but I did. That's why I sent you to the sub shop. And now because I saved you, you owe me."

I didn't owe that asshole jack. Time to wrap this fun little lunch right up.

I stood to leave. Yeah, he definitely looked amused now.

"Luca, I don't have much money, but I'll give you what I have. I've been saving it to move my little sister out here, but if you really want it, you can have it—"

He frowned and cut me off. "Do I look like I need money?"

Well, no.

"You have to come home with me," he said, polishing off the last oyster and looking mighty smug.

"Yeah. I don't think so," I said. "But thanks for the invite."

Dick.

This was where I'd have doubled over laughing if I hadn't been so damn scared of the man.

"You have to come live with my brother and me for a three-month period, and play what we call 'The Game.' After that, you are free to go."

At that, I actually did burst out laughing just as some sort of soup was delivered. Luca picked up his spoon and dove in.

"Yeah, that's a good one, Luca. Hilarious. But I gotta go now. Thanks for the clothes."

As I stood, I turned and leaned into his face. "And thanks for killing everyone at my club, you fucking asshole."

His hand found my wrist, and it tightened like a vise.

"This is not a joke," he said.

Oh. Crap. I tried to pull out of his grip, to no avail.

"You will have your own room in our home, and you don't have to do anything you don't want to."

I waved my free hand for him to stop. "You don't understand. I have to work. I have to support myself and my sister. In fact, I need to go find a new job since everyone at my old job is now *dead*."

Again, he shook his head at me. "You don't need to work."

Yeah, right.

"You will be provided for, as will your sister."

For the second time, I burst out laughing.

"I'm serious. You will be supported by us, and very generously, at that."

Okay. I go from cocktailing in a shitty dive strip club to being a prisoner of the two gorgeous twins of organized crime?

I was speechless.

What was I going to tell my roommate, Yasmina?

Luca got up from his side of the booth, still gripping my wrist, and pushed me back into my seat. I was effectively trapped. That's when he let go.

And damn if he didn't smell great.

Which reminded me.

"Luca, was that weird smell at the club this morning… from guns or something?"

He picked up a lock of my hair and brought it to his nose. "Yeah. That was from the guns."

And don't you know, while he twisted a lock of my hair around his forefinger, he leaned toward me, right there in the restaurant, and brushed his lips across mine.

It was as though I'd put my finger in an electrical outlet. Tingles shot through my every pore. And while I knew I was supposed to hate the guy, something made me lean toward him for more.

God, I was in trouble.

Big trouble.

CHAPTER 11

ECHO

I DIDN'T UTTER a word on the way to Luca's house. I mean, what the hell could I say? The guy claimed I 'owed him,' which of course was total bullshit, but I was in no position to make a break and run.

At least not yet. I had to get the lay of the land. These Borroni dudes didn't mess around. Just ask my boss, Bob.

Yeah, my dead boss, Bob.

We pulled into the crunchy, circular driveway of a big modern house built into the side of a hill on the outskirts of town. Crime pays, it would seem.

The place reminded me of something Frank Lloyd Wright might have designed. All crazy flying angles, but at the same time, retiring, as if the structure were meant to be there. It fit perfectly into the desert landscape.

Floor-to-ceiling glass stretched across the front of the home, and all I could think about was how damn hot it must get in the Vegas sun.

Their summer air conditioning bills must be insane.

"This where you live?" I asked, looking at a small collection of black SUVs parked around the side of the house.

What did they have, a damn army?

"Yup. Me, my brother, and various staff."

Staff?

"C'mon, I'll show you your room," he said, taking me by the hand.

But I didn't want to see my room. I didn't even *want* a room. I wanted to go home to the dumpy little apartment I shared with Yasmina, and call it a day. A long day, and a day I'd prefer to forget.

Luca reached for my hand, but I crossed my arms before he could get hold of me. I didn't want him to think for a moment I was going into this bullshit willingly.

We entered a cavernous foyer, because what else would you have if you're a successful criminal, and he led me up a wide, open plan staircase that looked like it was floating. I stuck to the left because that was the only side with a bannister.

"Here's your room. What do you think? You like it?"

he asked, pushing open a set of double doors at the end of a hallway.

I did a complete three-sixty to take in the room—the room that was to be mine for the three months I was 'paying back' him and his twin.

It was nice.

Actually, who was I kidding?

It was fucking awesome.

Damn those guys, for giving me a room to die for.

"Wow," I muttered, walking to the four-poster queen bed and smoothing my hand over the faux-fur throw tossed across it.

I plopped down and pulled off my new boots and socks to run my bare toes through the plushy rug. Damn if it didn't feel amazing.

It was like they had somehow spied on my Pinterest boards to find the objects of my bohemian desires and planted them in a room in their mansion just for me.

Hmmm.

Had they actually done that? I wouldn't put it past them.

It was perfection.

There was no other word for it. Pure perfection.

But it didn't matter, because I wasn't sticking around. Fuck this place. They thought they could win me over with a pretty bedroom? What kind of idiot did they think I was?

Luca was smiling, like he was proud of himself.

Wait 'til I hit the road. We'd see how much he was smiling then.

But for the short—very short—period of time I'd be there, I could appreciate the comforts the room afforded. I just wouldn't get used to them.

I wandered over to a little vanity covered with several perfume bottles and packages of brand-new, never-opened makeup and nail polish.

Had they raided Sephora or something?

The vanity also held a phone charger. The *exact* phone charger my cell required.

Interesting.

There was a seating area across the room drowning in cushy pillows and throws, and a giant palm tree whose leaves fanned over the furniture like shade on a tropical veranda. For all the time I'd be spending lounging about, no doubt.

"Where do these go?" I asked, getting ready to pull open two double doors.

"Open them."

So I did.

Jesus.

It was every girl's dream-come-true closet. Rows and rows of shelves for shoes, two giant dressers, and hanging space that would rival any boutique. There was a full-length mirror and dimmer switches on the lights. You could see what you'd look like in the daylight or nighttime.

The damn thing was about as big as the apartment I shared with Yasmina.

I pulled the doors shut. No sense in getting excited.

"Big closet. Too bad I only have like three pair of shoes and enough clothes to fill a small suitcase."

It was still nice to look at, even if it would remain empty.

"You have a private bathroom, too."

Holy shit, I hadn't even considered that I'd have my own bath.

I ran to the room's other closed door. I put my hand on the brass knob.

"Is this it?" I asked.

Luca just smiled.

So I pushed the door open to find a vintage claw-foot tub, a huge stand-up shower, and a deep granite sink. Hanging plants dangled long vines of ivy from the ceiling almost to the floor, giving the room a tropical, outdoorsy feel.

"Lovely," I said in a small voice.

I wasn't going to be swayed by nice digs. I mean, how big of an idiot did they think I was? *Give her a nice room, that'll shut her up.*

I don't think so.

Luca flicked a switch on the wall and fairy lights hanging from the bed posts lit up. It was like I'd entered some freaky sort of universe that was perfect and beautiful. And it was mine. For three months.

Not.

CHAPTER 12

ECHO

"Mr. Luca, you have a delivery."

I whipped around, not having realized we weren't alone in the house.

I guess when you had a home of this size, you needed to fill it with people. Or something like that.

A woman in a housekeeper's dress and sensible black shoes stood in the doorway to my room, looking me up and down. And not in a good way.

Her brow was furrowed, clearly disapproving of something.

I glanced down to see if I had something on my shirt.

"Thanks, Mary," Luca said. "Please have everything brought up here to Echo's room."

Echo's room. Pfffft.

Mary took a second to side eye me one more time. "Thank you, sir. I'll take care of it."

She disappeared.

"Friendly, isn't she?"

He laughed. "Oh, she's just super protective of my brother and me. She's been with the family… well, for a long time."

Before I could cross the room to check out the view from the windows, two new people barged into the room—*my* room, I guess—their arms piled high with garment bags. Close on their heels was a guy pushing a hand truck laden with several boxes.

They went straight into my closet and began filling it up. I'd never seen anything like that. I couldn't wear all those clothes if I lived to be a hundred.

I moved closer to Luca and lowered my voice. "What's going on?"

He gestured toward the closet. "You needed some things to wear, right?"

"Um, I usually like to choose my own clothes."

"Oh, you'll like these things. Don't worry."

Whatever.

Luca and I watched the trio work in fast motion, and in less than five minutes they'd loaded up the closet and split, returning to wherever they'd come from without having spoken a word.

Shit was just getting weirder. It was like *Stepford Wives* for criminals.

Except they called it The Game.

"Good lord," I said, looking at the newly filled racks, shelves, and drawers.

I knew I should have said thank you. But I was too pissed for that.

"We wanted you to be comfortable. Hey, I'm going to leave you now. I have some work to do, and I'm sure you'd like to get settled in. If you need anything, holler. Mary will be able to get you anything you want to eat, and I'll be in my office downstairs."

He walked toward me, and I stiffened.

Look, I wasn't an idiot. A guy doesn't give you shit like this without expecting something in return.

But all he did was lightly kiss my temple and leave, pulling the door closed behind him.

Incredulous, I looked around the room again. It was my boho dream come true, even if I were a fucking prisoner.

Leaning my ear against the door, I listened as Luca's footsteps retreated. I turned the lock on the knob.

There.

I knew, of course, that anyone could get into my room if they really wanted to. But I wasn't going to make it easy.

Maybe I should slide a chair against the door, before I went to sleep. A girl couldn't be too careful.

Gorgeous bedroom notwithstanding, I was in a house with strangers. Sure, I'd sort of known Luca and his brother Leo from Loaded Dice, and served them drinks every time they'd come in, but I didn't *know* them beyond saying hello. I barely knew what they did for a living, except it seemed to involve killing people. Or getting other people to kill *for* them. Unfortunate people like my boss, Bob, who either didn't understand how the game was played or thought he did and had been wrong. I felt terrible for him—he'd been so kind to me in the couple of weeks I'd worked there.

A wave of exhaustion poured over me. It had been a fucked-up day, and the champagne I'd consumed at my late lunch hadn't exactly perked me up.

In spite of my efforts to resist being seduced by my fancy surroundings, the bed looked deliciously inviting. But before I could even consider crawling in, I needed to get the lay of the land, at least to the extent that I could.

And I needed to call Yasmina.

She picked up on the first ring.

"Hey, are ya busy?" I asked.

"Oh, hey, girl. How's your day? Are you off work yet?" she asked. "I just finished my last cut and blow dry. Whew, it was a long day. You done with work yet?"

She thought it was funny that a cocktail waitress would work a day shift, like a regular office worker. It *was* kind of funny, when I thought about it.

"Yes, I'm done for the day. It was… kind of a rough one." I didn't know where to begin explaining the odyssey I'd been through. I plopped down in the velvet chair in front of my vanity. I didn't dare sit on the bed for fear of falling asleep.

"Oh shit, sorry to hear that."

She didn't know the half of it.

"Want to meet up for drinks in a bit?" she asked.

Was I allowed to do that?

"I don't… think I can."

"Why the hell not? You too tired?"

I nodded, even though she couldn't see me. "I am tired, yes. Exhausted, actually. Look, I just wanted to tell you I won't be home tonight."

She giggled. "Oh, *that's* what you're up to. My girl's gonna get some nookie. Awesome, sweetie, it's been way too long for you."

She was right that it *had* been a long time, but I didn't think that particular issue was going to be resolved anytime soon. At least not that I knew of.

"Okay then, have a good night," I said.

Once I'd gotten that out of the way—because there was no underestimating the worry that not hearing from me would cause Yasmina—I could now take care of my second order of business.

I returned to my giant closet, which was now nearly full, thanks to the silent people who'd breezed in and filled it up. I pulled open one of the dresser drawers and found the softest cotton pajamas.

Yeah. I'd be wearing these babies, and real soon.

Pajamas. It was so odd to be doing something so normal in such an abnormal situation.

I clutched the jammies to my chest and examined every nook and cranny of the closet in case I needed a hiding place at some point. There really wasn't much to speak of, except for a door in the ceiling overhead that I'd spotted, which I assumed led to an attic of sorts.

I made a mental note to explore that more, later.

It was only in movies that people hid in closets, anyway, right? I mean, wasn't that the first place the bad guys always looked?

Then, I snooped around the rest of the room, looking for what, I wasn't sure. It wasn't like I'd be able to identify hidden cameras or recording devices, but I wanted to look, just the same.

I wandered into the bathroom to check out the collection of high-end skincare products they'd provided. I washed up and tossed my dirty clothes on the closet floor. I could take care of that shit later. Or a housekeeper would.

Oh my god. A housekeeper might be picking up my clothes.

Yeah, don't get used to it, sister.

When I flicked off my lights, a strange glow flooded my bedroom. I walked over to the double doors opening to a small balcony and spotted Luca in the backyard by an illuminated swimming pool. He had a cigar in one hand and a drink in the other. He was just getting up from a lounge chair, where I guess he'd been hanging out, and walked to the edge of the pool.

Where he pulled his shirt off over his head and dropped his pants to his ankles.

Leaving him butt naked.

Oh.

I stepped to the side of the window to hide in case he decided to turn and look up at my room, and watched him slowly walk around the pool after setting his smoke and drink on a small table.

And he was beautiful.

Of course.

His rock-hard ass flexed with every step he took, and his broad shoulders looked like they could take down anyone who looked at him wrong. And when he turned, I had a perfect view of the long cock hanging between his legs.

Ohmygod.

I ducked back behind the window, trying to catch my breath. A splash broke the silence, as he dove in and began swimming long, graceful laps.

When he was done, he pulled himself up out of the pool, slicking his hair back with his hands. He was even more gorgeous, if that were possible, with his skin shiny and wet. He picked up his drink and cigar and headed back to the house, leaving his clothes behind.

Guess cleaning up stuff like that was part of Mary's job description.

My heart was still pounding when I crawled under the fluffy down comforter on my bed and flicked off the fairy lights above me.

As tired as I was, I wasn't beyond a little self-plea-sure in spite of my bizarre surroundings. I slipped my hand down my PJ pants and got to work, imagining skinny-dipping but with Luca looking out his window at *me* instead.

I'd slowly undress, folding my clothes on the lounge chair. Then, I'd walk over to the edge of the pool and bend deeply to run my fingers through the water. When I was satisfied it was a nice temperature, I'd dive in and float on my back giving him a perfect view of all I had to offer.

I worked my clit faster and faster as I pictured myself putting on a show for him and maybe even his brother, when I came so hard, I forgot to keep my moans down.

Shit.

Was someone at my door?

Perfectly quiet, I held still and heard soft footsteps retreating.

Oops. Busted.

CHAPTER 13

ECHO

NEXT MORNING, I decided to hold my head high even though someone in the house had heard my little self-pleasure, and went downstairs in my PJs and a robe Luca's minions had thoughtfully left in my closet.

I stopped at the entrance to the dining room, when I saw Luca and a strange man sitting at the table.

"You must be Echo," the new guy said, in possibly the deepest voice I'd ever heard.

Luca, looking up from the newspaper he was reading, turned the page, and said nothing.

Good morning to you too, asshole.

"Hi. Yes, I am."

The man nodded at me. Still nothing from Luca.

"I'm Smitt. Please have a seat." He gestured at the large, mostly empty table.

I scooted over and sat, red with embarrassment. Why hadn't I thought to get dressed?

Mary bustled into the dining room, presumably from the kitchen. "Coffee's over there," she said, gesturing with her chin at the room's sideboard.

Guess that meant I'd get my own.

No biggie. I was a freaking waitress, after all.

She set a large platter of eggs, sausage, and biscuits on the table and disappeared.

"This looks awesome," Smitt said, diving in.

Still nothing from Luca.

That's when Leo entered. I'd not seen him since the previous morning and the 'incident.'

I hoped he might be friendlier than Luca.

But he only winked at me, grabbed some coffee, and left.

Luca made a sudden movement, closing his news-paper and looking at his watch. He reached for his coffee cup and taking one more gulp, stood, pushed his chair back in, and left just like Leo had.

Without a word.

Weird fucking place.

I dug into the eggs and sausage. I was starving, and to hell with those guys if they couldn't be friendly in the morning.

I was a grown-ass woman and could deal with their games. It wasn't like I'd be there for long, anyway.

Not that they knew that.

"What do you do here, Smitt?" I asked. Perhaps I could get him on my side. I needed an ally.

He adjusted the collar around his large neck.

Seriously, I'd thought the twins were big men, but this guy was gigantic.

"Security. Stuff like that."

Stuff like that. I wanted to know what kind of *stuff like that* but the expression on his face indicated it was better not to ask.

He looked at me with a nice smile. "So, you wanna take a swim or something? Luca told me there's a bathing suit for you in your room."

"Oh. I guess I could do that. Hey, do you think you could give me a ride somewhere?"

He frowned. "Not likely."

I should have seen that coming.

"Why not?" I asked.

"Well, the guys want you to stay here. It's safer for you."

Safer?

"What if I leave on my own? I could just call an Uber," I said.

He shrugged. "That's true. You could. I won't stop you. But the consequences might not be pretty."

What the fuck did that mean?

"If you get bored, there's a gym in the basement, and a really nice library. Lots of cool books in there."

Oh wow. Libraries had books?

Did he think I was a dumbass?

"Smitt," I said, leaning toward him, "am I a prisoner here?"

He furrowed his brow. "I wouldn't put it like that, Echo."

"Am I Luca and Leo's whore, then?"

Surprise splashed across his face. "Well, everybody's a whore to one extent or another."

Holy shit. A philosopher security man. This week was getting weirder by the moment.

Back in my room, I dug through a couple of drawers until I found the bathing suit Smitt had referred to. It was a navy blue one-piece, low-cut in the front but elegant in its simplicity. I didn't know the designer on the label so looked it up on Google.

The fucker cost five hundred dollars. A *bathing suit*.

I was half-tempted to try and return it for the cash. But I couldn't leave so nixed the idea.

I looked around my beautiful room, wondering if these four walls, and actually all the house's walls, were the only ones I'd see during my supposed three months there.

Could I just be a lady of leisure with nothing more to do than sit by the pool, work out, and read books?

Maybe, maybe not. But it beat serving cocktails in a strip club, however temporary.

CHAPTER 14

LUCA

LEO STOOD in the doorway of my office at our business headquarters wearing his usual smirk, then wandered in to help himself to the chair opposite my desk. As usual, he propped his feet up of top of a pile of papers, showing off the soles of his very expensive shoes.

Busy staff bustled back and forth outside my door. Just how I liked it.

And, as usual, I got annoyed. "Do you have to put your goddamn feet on my desk?"

He frowned and shifted them back to the floor where they belonged. "What's up with you? Got your period?"

"Fuck off," I said, smiling.

Leo sighed. "So, I wasn't sure things were going to go as planned yesterday at Loaded Dice. That was some close-call shit. I almost didn't get the dancers out in time, and then when the guys got to work, I thought they might have tipped off old Bob with the way he went running behind the bar. I was sure he was going for his firearms."

"Look, the guy knew he was in the dog house, and must have figured that at some point things were going to get lethal. I'm surprised he wasn't armed already."

I pulled up the local news on my computer. "Nothing in the news, yet. Guess the family's connections are paying off."

Leo shook his head. "Yup, no news is good news, huh?"

"So, how did you get the dancers out?" I asked.

He leaned forward, elbows on knees. "Well, there were only two of them, fortunately, and one was already heading out. The other one—the young one who'd been dancing for us—started asking questions, but the older dancer shut her right down. I gave them each a few hundos, told them to forget we'd ever spoken, and to haul ass out of there and not look back."

"Do you think they're gonna talk?"

He shook his head again. "No way. They're not idiots. I mean, the young one was kind of green, but she got the gist of my message. She'll go find a new job, hopefully at a better place, and forget she ever danced at Loaded Dice."

That made me feel better.

"These dancers, they see some shit, don't they?"

It was true. They were on the front line of Vegas's seedy underside and had to become experts at staying out of the line of fire. I'd seen more than one fight break out in strip clubs, usually due to alcohol intoxication. Dancers and cocktail waitresses alike knew to get the hell out of the way as fast as possible, and to make themselves scarce while tensions were soothed.

They didn't call it the 'Wild West' for nothing.

"Everyone in Vegas got our message loud and clear after the hit, that's for sure," I said.

I didn't particularly like having people taken out, but when our hand was forced—we had no choice. If we didn't react with swift, firm action, it would set a dangerous precedent even I didn't want to think about.

"Don't look so serious, big bro," Leo said. "If people weren't such fuckups, we wouldn't have to do this shit."

I glanced out my floor-to-ceiling windows overlooking the Strip and the dusty high desert mountains beyond it.

"So do you think the girl will stay quiet?" he asked, changing the subject.

I turned back to my brother. "Her name is *Echo*. And yes, I think she will."

I knew what was coming next.

"How long 'til we start The Game?"

I picked up a pen and hit it against my desk.

Tap, tap, tap.

I looked at Leo, which was just like looking in the

mirror save for my facial hair. People asked me all the time if it was weird, having an identical twin.

But how could I answer that? I'd never known anything else.

He'd always been there. There was no memory of life without him.

Which was both good and bad. Sometimes we loved each other. Sometimes we hated each other.

And now I was starting to get a headache, as I often did when pressured by him.

"Not sure. I'm moving slowly with this one. She's… I don't know… green. She's green."

"Oh for Christ's sake, Luca. You like her. You've liked her since you first saw her. This won't work. It won't work."

Fucking A.

"Would you calm down, Leo? I told you I'm moving slowly. I don't care about the conclusions you're drawing. They're your problem, not mine. I'm primary, here."

Times like this made me seriously reconsider the affection I had for my brother, who rolled his eyes and turned to leave just as another visitor arrived.

CHAPTER 15

LUCA

"Well, here they are, the dynamic duo. Hey, I need to talk to you guys."

Sal Matteo, the leader of our syndicate, made himself at home in the seat Leo had just vacated.

"What's up, Sal? Everything good?" Leo asked.

Sal and our father had run what they called 'the family business' together for years. But one day, when we were eighteen, Pops just didn't come home. Never heard from him again. He'd disappeared, right into thin air. That's when Leo and I stepped into his shoes. We were technically 'equal' in authority to Sal, but we deferred to him out of respect. *Most* of the time. In many ways, he was like a second father to us. He had even looked out for our mother, at least until she was murdered.

Shit. Every time I thought of that, it was like a new punch to the gut.

He leaned back in his chair, hands behind his head like he didn't have a care in the world. Which meant he was about to drop a bomb.

"All good, and good job on the Loaded Dice situation. Sometimes it's best to cut your losses and run. Sends an important message to all our associates," he said.

That was the idea, anyway.

He continued. "So, there's a band of assholes we've found who are cheating at cards all over town. They've unfortunately made the grave mistake of doing this at *our* casinos."

Damn. Not a smart move. Sal was the king of *zero tolerance*. He was both respected and feared for it. At least by smart folks.

"These guys are local, and they should know better than to piss off the wrong people." Sal shook his head regretfully. "They're gonna have to be taught a lesson."

I knew what that meant, and unfortunately for the card counters, it was seriously bad news.

Sal droned on about how they'd discovered the guys, and how he wanted them dealt with, but I was only half listening. I knew Leo would get the gist of what was going down and fill in me in on any missed information later.

Leo's mention of Echo had put her on my mind again, front and center. Problem was, this time I couldn't get her *off* my mind, and thinking about her curvy ass and tits had me going to the point where I hoped I wouldn't have to stand up, and least not while there were other people in the room.

I preferred for Sal and Leo to remain unaware of my growing erection.

"—and we have to tread carefully here. Some of the kids involved in this scam are connected to our business partners. I want to see this put to an end, at least in our casinos, but without starting a full-on war."

"We could make it look like the hit came from the Russians on the other side of town," I offered.

Sal nodded. "I thought of that, too, but you know how crazy those bastards are. They don't just shoot someone in the head and be done with it. They drag shit out because they're sadistic motherfuckers."

"We'll suss out the situation, Sal," Leo promised.

"I knew I could count on my boys to take care of business. I'm lucky to have the two of you," he said.

I could swear there was a tear in his eyes.

Leo patted him on the back as he made his way to the door. "We're always here for you, Sal."

What could I say? If Sal told us to jump off a cliff, we'd probably do it.

We'd probably never know exactly what sort of an untimely end our father may have met, whether he left the country to go into hiding, or possibly entered the witness protection program. The main thing was we sure as shit never saw or heard from him again.

So, we were nothing if not indebted to Sal.

When he was gone, Leo sat back down. "Well, this'll keep us busy for a while. Seriously, why do people pull that shit? They know someone will catch up with them at some point."

I didn't get it, either. I mean, card counters played as long as they could and usually disappeared when things got too hot. But these guys were blatant—a fatal mistake. They'd pulled the tail of a tiger, pissing Sal off, and they were about to see what it was like to have their heads bitten off.

Metaphorically, of course.

"So. You going to the club tonight?" Leo asked.

Ugh. That was about the last thing I wanted to do. I knew Echo was home, not necessarily waiting for me, but waiting for *something*. Smitt had been instructed to keep her there all day, and by the time I got home, she'd probably be on the verge of going stir-crazy.

I shook my head.

Leo dropped his head back and roared with laughter.

Dick.

"You have a hard-on for that girl. I knew it!"

"Fuck off, Leo."

"Okay then. Why are you stalling on kicking off The Game? What good is there in waiting? If you don't think she's right, get rid of her."

I couldn't even look at him.

He was right. And I didn't like it.

We never kept women around who weren't right for us. But I didn't know yet about Echo. It was too soon to tell.

"Get out of my office, please. I have work to do."

He shook his head disdainfully. "I knew you were pussy-whipped by her. Luca, you know I don't like it when this happens."

He walked toward my office door, but before closing it behind himself, he turned to me one last time.

"Break her in, Luca. Get her ready. I'm serious."

He pulled the door closed, and not a moment too soon. I wanted to wring his frigging neck.

CHAPTER 16

LUCA

THE PROBLEM with having a twin is that you know every fucking thing about each other. He knew he was about to push me too far. And I knew he had a point about the girl.

The very girl I wanted to be with tonight, instead of going to the club with my brother, as we usually did a couple of times a week.

Yeah, I was done for the day. I wasn't able to concentrate, and when I was, all I could think about was Echo. Luca was right. I did have a goddamn hard-on for her. Literally. Just like I'd had the night before when I'd sneaked into her room to watch her sleeping.

Yeah, I'd actually done that.

I'd glimpsed her watching me get my evening swim, so made sure she had a good eyeful of my naked ass before turning in. I guess my plan worked, because when I walked past her room on the way to mine, I heard quiet moaning.

My girl needed some dick.

Christ. Did I just say *my girl*?

I'd hustled on down the hall to my own room since I was dripping from the pool, but later found I couldn't sleep, even after I jacked it in a long, hot shower. I got back out of bed to head downstairs to the kitchen for something to eat, but couldn't get past Echo's door.

What was it about her?

I knew I shouldn't, but I reached for her doorknob.

And it was locked.

Fortunately for me, the skeleton key I needed was tucked into the trim at the top of her door.

I placed it in the lock and twisted it, making no noise save for a couple *clicks* and walked into her room.

Yeah, I was that kind of an asshole.

She was lying on her side in the new pajamas the crew had brought over, with a column of light passing over her, probably from the moon reflecting on the swimming pool outside her open window.

Wow. She slept with a window open. A woman after my own heart.

I silently walked up to the end of her bed and found her breathing deeply, her hair strewn over the pillow behind her, and one hand under her cheek.

But I had a start when she sighed loudly and flipped to her other side. I thought for sure I'd been caught.

Instead, her bed began to slightly rock and she made a few whimpering noises.

Goddamn if she wasn't rubbing herself under the covers.

Which instantly gave me a boner.

I lowered my pajama bottoms and pulled out my erection, stroking it from root to tip in time to her strokes. I was dying to climb into bed with her.

Patience, dickhead, patience.

Just before coming, I tucked myself back in my pants and left the room, pulling the door closed behind me. I didn't bother locking it. I wanted to give her something to wonder about.

Back in my room, I jerked myself until I came harder than I had in a long time, the whole time picturing my dick sliding back and forth between Echo's cushy ass cheeks. It was such a fucking hot release that I turned over and slept right through 'til morning, when Mary knocked on my door to get me up.

And now, at the office, I was just as fucking horny as I'd been eighteen hours before. In no shape to get behind the wheel of my Tesla, I slipped into the private bathroom in my office and took care of business, again with Echo front and center in my mind.

Now, I was ready to head home to her.

On the way out, I passed Leo's office but didn't even pause to say goodbye.

I had more important things to tend to.

CHAPTER 17

ECHO

Luca met me at the entrance to the dining room, handed me a glass of wine, and kissed me on the temple.

Just like he had the day before. Only this time, I didn't flinch.

"You look amazing," he breathed.

Well, that was a different tune from the morning's treatment. But I guess this shit was called The Game for a reason.

And he didn't look too bad himself, still in his bespoke work clothes.

Earlier, he'd called me from his office and asked me to wear a dress he'd just had sent over. Not five minutes later, the doorbell rang, and Mary screamed for me from the front hallway.

I'd considered ignoring her, partly to irritate her but mostly to teach her how *not* to treat me. I mean, if I was supposed to be there for three months, I didn't want them to be three long, miserable months at the hands of a grumpy cook and housekeeper. But in the end, she'd hollered that a package had come. I was a ho for surprises, so I ran down the stairs to collect my goods like a bratty kid on Christmas morning.

Naturally, I wouldn't grant Mary the satisfaction of opening the box in front of her, even though she was watching with expectation. I ran back up to my room and closed the door, locking it. I figured I couldn't be too safe. Funny thing was, the night before I could have sworn I'd locked it before going to bed, but when I got up in the morning, it was unlocked. Closed, but unlocked.

Maybe I'd turned the latch in the wrong direction. *Note to self: next time, make sure the door's actually locked.*

I laid the box on my bed and began scrambling through layer after layer of deep blue tissue paper. For a moment, I wondered if there was anything inside the box, but when I saw that what was inside was so close to the color of the paper, I realized I'd nearly missed it.

I reached for the blue fabric in the bottom of the box, and a long garment of heavy, expensive silk washed through my hands. I'd never felt something so soft yet weighty. I gathered it into my hands and dashed into my closet to stand in front of the full-length mirror.

Holding it to my chest, I could see Luca had sent me a simple but stunning gown with a halter-style top and straight skirt that reached to the floor, with a long slit up the thigh.

It was stunning. Exactly what I would have imagined for myself had someone asked what I envisioned in an evening dress—but far more beautiful because I'd never even seen an evening dress in person, much less owned or worn one.

How did he do that?

My phone buzzed, and I jumped.

you get the dress?

I texted him back a smiley emoji. That was it. I didn't want to seem *too* pleased. After all, I was still trying to make a prison break. Just biding my time.

Although with gifts like this, being a tough girl was going to be a challenge.

And now, I got to show off the dress—live and in person.

He had instructed me to meet him, wearing the new dress, in the dining room. I was so excited that I put it on just to walk around my room in it. I might have danced around a little, too.

I found a couple of YouTube videos for help with my hair and makeup, and I was good to go.

Even if I was an hour early for dinner. And, because I didn't want to wrinkle the dress, I watched a couple episodes of *Friends* standing up.

At the instructed time, I glided down the stairs, my stilettos *click-clicking*, announcing my arrival.

I couldn't deny it. I felt about as hot as a girl can get.

And from the way Luca stared at me, he might have thought the same. At least I hoped so.

After greeting me, he pulled my chair out at the dining table, the same place where, just that morning, he couldn't be bothered to say hello.

Taking a seat opposite, his gaze never left me. "The dress fits you perfectly."

I was suddenly nervous. Anyone would be under that intense stare.

His hazel eyes—neither green nor brown but somewhere in between—had a darkness about them that I wasn't sure how to read. But they were delicious, and full of passion—that I was sure of.

And then I got a funny *déjà vu* sensation. I'd dreamed of him the night before, where he was wearing pajama bottoms low on his hips, and a thin trail of hair starting at his belly button disappeared beneath the drawstring waist. I'd wanted to see more, but he'd just smiled and walked away.

Now that I thought back, it seemed so real.

I smoothed my dress over my lap, taking care not to step on it with my heels. "Thank you for the dress. I've never had anything like it."

Crap. I didn't mean to show my cards so fast. Oh well.

Mary came in with a tray, which she set down on a

sideboard. She served us each a huge Caesar salad, while grabbing the opportunity to give me as many dirty looks as she could squeeze into the few seconds she was in the dining room.

After she left, I whispered, "What's wrong with her?"

Luca rolled his eyes. "I saw that. I'll have a talk with her."

He pulled a phone out of his pocket and tapped the screen several times.

"Hey, Luc. You need something?" Smitt asked, appearing out of nowhere.

Luca nodded. "Hey, Smitt, would you send Mary home and finish up the night for her?"

He tipped his head pleasantly, and I smiled at him. He did seem like a nice guy.

"Sure, boss. I'll do it right now."

When he'd left the room, I whispered again. "What exactly does he do here?"

Luca laughed. "Good question. He does a bit of everything—security, driving, and sometimes he does butler kinds of duties."

I tried not to giggle. "So he's essentially your bitch?"

Luca smiled slightly. "Well, I don't know about that. He's a good guy. I've known him nearly all my life. We came up in the business together."

I almost asked *what kind of business* but reminded myself I didn't really want to know.

Mary must have been sent on her way, because

Smitt returned with another large tray. I grabbed my salad plate and stood, intending to take it and Luca's off the table and deliver it to the kitchen sink like all polite guests do.

But Luca raised his hands in the air signaling *sit back down.*

So I did, plate in hand.

"You don't have to do that. Smitt will get it."

"That's right, I will," he said, sweeping right in with a smile. He removed our salad plates and served filet mignon, sweet potato mash, and a bunch of other amazing-smelling dishes.

That was when I realized I'd not eaten since the morning, save for a handful of grapes. After breakfast I'd stayed out of Mary's way. The woman was fucking scary.

I sliced into my steak, and the first bite of tender meat melted in my mouth.

"Mmmm."

"You like that," Luca said when Smitt disappeared into the kitchen.

"Oh my god," I moaned. "I'm sorry. I'm just gobbling everything up, it's so good."

I took a deep breath when I'd cleaned my plate and was a little embarrassed to see Luca only halfway through his meal.

Whatever.

"So I have a question for you."

"Mmmm?" he murmured, eyebrows raised.

"When can I leave?"

He frowned almost imperceptibly, and set his fork down, taking a swig of soda water to finish his bite. He cleared his throat and wiped his mouth with a cloth napkin.

"Why would you want to leave?"

Seriously? Did he really just ask that?

"Well, I have a life to live. You know, I need to eventually get a new job since my old place of employment was, well, decimated. My sister is counting on me. And I can't just sit around the house all day long."

He tilted his head at me. "Why not?"

Was he joking?

Actually, I could see he wasn't. He was dead serious. He really didn't know why I'd want to do something *other* than sit around on my ass all day.

What kind of crazy universe did this guy live in?

And before I could answer, Smitt appeared with dessert. He swept our dinner plates away, leaving me feeling like a lazy bum, and set a huge apple pie and bowl of vanilla ice cream down in front of us.

Pie.

I momentarily forgot about my future. I was obsessed with pie. The bastard had identified my Achilles' heel.

I fucking *loved* pie.

"Oh, let me serve," I said, reaching for the dessert plates Smitt had set out.

"Thank you," Luca said.

I cut enormous slices, because that's how I roll, and plopped equally generous scoops of ice cream on each.

I dove in like a starved animal.

"Oh. My. God," I said. "Un-fucking believable."

I was eating like a pig, and I didn't care.

"Slow down, you'll make yourself sick."

He didn't know me. I never got sick. At least not like that.

And who was he anyway? My mother?

He walked around to my side of the table, snatching my fork and grabbing a napkin to dab the corners of my mouth.

"What are you doing? I wasn't finished," I whined, trying to steal back my fork.

But he held it out of my reach. "Relax. I'm not taking anything away from you."

I eyed my fork and then side-eyed him, hoping he'd connect the dots.

I supposed I could eat with my fingers if I had to. I'd done worse.

"Let me feed you."

Ohforchristssake. Weirdo.

"Open," he said quietly, his gaze transfixed on my mouth.

Hmmm. Could this be fun?

I licked my lips lightly and then parted them—but not enough for him to feed me.

Why make it easy?

He smiled at my rebellion, running his fingers along my jaw and then down my neck.

Then grabbed a fistful of my hair.

"Ow!" I wailed.

He'd not only gripped my hair but with a small yank, pulled my head back into an angled position. It was not comfortable.

But I guess that was the point.

"Open," he demanded with another yank.

I looked down at the fork heading for my mouth, and it was piled with enough pie and ice cream for two or three mouthfuls.

And it was getting closer.

"Wider," he growled.

I opened, and he stuffed my mouth with so much pie and ice cream that half of it dribbled back down my chin and onto the table.

I sputtered and swallowed what I could. "Hey. Look at the mess you made." I reached for my napkin and drew it to my face.

But he whipped it out of my hand and threw it to the floor.

"Open," he said again.

I'd had about enough so pressed my lips together and shook my head. I didn't want to get anything on my dress, among other things.

But with a yank of my hair, my mouth opened, and he loaded me up again.

"That's enough," I said, as soon as I'd swallowed.

Luca threw the fork on the table, and while he continued to grip my hair, he pressed his lips to mine, smearing the mess from my face to his.

He didn't give a shit.

And neither did I.

His free hand wandered up my bare arm, then down the front of my dress, where he began to knead one of my breasts. With his other hand, he opened the dress clasp behind my neck. The halter top fell forward, and I was bare.

He smiled. "Look at these amazing tits. You know how beautiful you are, Echo?"

But I couldn't answer. His mouth was on mine.

That's when the door between the dining room and kitchen squeaked open. I tore myself back from Luca and covered my chest.

Smitt had come to clean the dishes off the sideboard.

I looked at Luca in alarm.

"Don't worry about him." He pushed my arms out of the way, burying his head between my breasts.

These people were kinky fuckers.

Smitt disappeared as fast as he'd appeared, without even looking our way.

Luca grabbed his napkin and dabbed it in his water glass. He rubbed it over my mouth and chin to remove the ice cream remnants and did the same to himself. Then he stood, taking my hand, and pulled me up. He laid me back on the table, pushing my legs up on the edge so I was spread open.

Oh. My. God. In the freaking dining room?

"Beautiful," he whispered after he'd slipped my dress aside and lowered my thong panty.

Kisses tickled the insides of my thighs before his tongue parted my pussy lips, running from my clit to ass and back. I squirmed under his touch and pushed up and into his face for more pressure.

I wanted more. A lot more.

I'd tried to resist. But it just didn't work.

"Oh god, Luca," I murmured, "I'm gonna come."

He put his arms under my thighs and pushed them up until they hurt, working my clit with a suction that left me pounding my fists on the table and writhing while one orgasm rolled over me, followed by another.

I heard his belt and pants open and fall to the floor while he tore a piece of plastic and rolled on a condom. He pulled me to the edge of the table until my ass was nearly hanging off it and notched himself at my opening.

"You ready, baby? You want my cock?"

Holyfuckingshit.

I nodded.

But I would have begged if I'd had to.

I'd never experienced anything so hot. A gorgeous man between my legs, who had propped me open on a dining room table. Anyone could walk in at any minute and the anticipation of that tripled my excitement.

He entered me halfway, and when I began to play with my tits, he plunged all the way in, throwing me into another set of orgasms that rolled over me until he hollered.

"Fuck, baby. I'm coming," he growled.

He lowered his head to my chest and pumped me a few more times with such a fury that if he hadn't been holding on to me, I would have flown off the table.

"Holy Christ," he murmured, collapsing on top of me.

Shit. This sort of fun was going to be hard to leave behind.

CHAPTER 18

ECHO

By the time I woke the next morning, the house was dead quiet. I tiptoed around the place in my fluffy Ugg slippers.

But there was no one home.

I wasn't sure whether I should be scared or excited. I had the place to myself.

And my mind was racing with the possibilities.

I'd go shopping. Smitt had said not to leave, but he was nowhere to be found.

I threw myself together as quickly as I could and called an Uber to take me to the mall. Now that I knew Luca *in the biblical sense*, I was sure he trusted me to fill my days however I wanted.

And I planned to, after I had a small taste of freedom.

It's not like I had a better plan. Yet.

The first thing I did was head to the food court for a vanilla milkshake and then head to the high-end department stores. I'd never spent much time in any of them before, but now, with the nice new clothes Luca had gotten me, I walked in like I owned the place.

And I clearly looked the part because everyone was asking if I needed help.

But I wasn't only turning the heads of the store employees. There seemed to be a couple guys—big guys—who were keeping an eye on me, too.

Were they sent by Luca? Or somebody else?

Was this going to be my life for three months, or as long as I stuck with The Game? I couldn't do anything without being monitored? Because I was not down with that. I was independent and enjoyed my own company. I didn't need or want babysitters.

How did my life get to this point, anyway? All I'd wanted to do was provide a way for my sister to join me in Las Vegas, out of the clutches of our horrible, neglectful mother, who hadn't actually raised us anyway.

My longer-term dream, far-fetched as it might be, was to open a little breakfast diner like the one I'd grown up going to. Just a small, old-school joint that attracted regulars and tourists alike, with booths and counter seating, and the best pies in town.

Because I loved pie.

Yeah, like that would ever happen.

As I went from rack to rack touching the expensive merchandise in the store, I wondered if I should have just stayed in my little shithole of a town. I mean, I almost had, that's how much I hated to leave my sister. But between the two of us, we'd decided I had more opportunity in a place like Vegas, and that once I'd saved enough money, she would join me.

But if I'd stayed in West Virginia, I wouldn't be in the position I was now, trying to 'pay back' two brothers—regardless of how drop-dead gorgeous they were—for supposedly saving my life.

Shit. I remembered I needed to check in with Yasmina.

On a quiet bench, I tapped my phone screen.

"Echo! Guess who just left our apartment?" she asked.

My stomach fell.

"Um… who?"

"Two big guys who were looking for you. Very good-looking and buff. I almost asked them in." She giggled.

I was surprised she *didn't* ask them in.

"I told them I had no idea where you were, which is actually true. They believed me and left. Are you still shacking up with some hottie? When you comin' home? And why would anyone be looking for you?"

I ignored her questions, looking over my shoulder at the big guys on my tail. "Look, Yasmina, I am not sure who those guys were, so be careful, okay? Don't invite strangers into our house."

Like she would ever listen to me.

A car door slammed on the other end of the line, and I looked at my watch. It was just about time for her to be getting to the salon.

She sighed. "Gotcha. But I can't make any promises. You know I like 'em big and burly."

"You're crazy. See ya," I said.

"Wait, wait," she said. "Seriously. Why were two men looking for you?"

Ugh.

"Um, Yas… can I call you later? I kind of have a long story to tell you."

"All right. But don't forget. You little *slut*," she screamed, laughing and then hanging up.

I might have managed to get out of the brothers' house, but I didn't feel nearly as free as I thought I would. With two guys following me and others knocking on my apartment door, I wasn't exactly foot-loose and fancy-free.

After an hour of aimless wandering, I was ready to go. With all the new stuff in my closet, I hardly needed to buy anything else—not that I had the money to anyway, especially since I was jobless. I pulled out my phone to get an Uber home. But when I looked up and saw the burly bodyguards, I had a better idea.

I wandered over to them. "Hey, you guys are here for me, right?" I asked.

They looked at each other, shifting uncomfortably.

"Well, yeah. We are," one of them said.

I smiled brightly. "Well, since we're all on the same team here, wanna give me a ride home, back to Luca's house? That would save me ten bucks on an Uber."

"Let's go," the other one said with a shrug.

CHAPTER 19

LUCA

UNNOTICED, I slipped out of the office for a little shopping at Tiffany. As I considered a variety of expensive items at the hands of a very patient saleswoman, who should walk by in the mall but freaking Echo. I nearly called out to her, but I didn't want her to know I was shopping at Tiffany, and second, I thought I'd just follow her for a bit.

And what was she doing outside the goddamn house, anyway?

With a beverage in hand, she looked cute as hell in the skinny jeans I'd gotten for her, and her slamming high-heeled boots made her shake her ass just enough as she click-clacked her way from one store window to the other.

She was just a beautiful woman, browsing the stores, without a care in the world.

Although I knew she had plenty of things on her mind. I still hadn't addressed her question about when she might be allowed to leave Leo and me. I wasn't in the mood to think about something like that when, all through dinner, I'd barely been able to take my eyes off the swell of her breasts that her gown showed off so perfectly.

I'd done well with that selection.

I kept a safe distance while I texted Smitt to send over a couple of security guys to take my place—I couldn't follow Echo around a mall all day. I had shit to do, and besides, I paid people to do stuff like that.

As soon as my guys arrived, I went back to Tiffany, although I wouldn't have minded looking at the lovely girl all day long. And I could have sent someone else to shop for me, like I usually did, but I needed to see the options in person to choose an appropriate gift.

A gift for Echo.

I'd actually imagined what sort of gift she might like the first time I saw her at Loaded Dice. She was so down-to-earth and real, I knew she was the kind of person who'd appreciate something pretty. I knew too many women who felt entitled, and there was no joy in being generous with people like that.

I settled on one of the traditional Tiffany key necklaces in platinum with embedded diamonds. It seemed like the perfect thing for Echo, representing the endless possibilities I knew she wanted for her life. And longed for so powerfully.

Funny thing, having such a sentiment about her. I didn't really even know her, although I was beginning to.

But the key would be gorgeous hanging from her neck, just above her delicious cleavage, with her thick black hair swirling around her shoulders.

God, I sounded like such a pussy.

When I'd first seen her bustling around Loaded Dice, trying to keep a bunch of drunk men happy and their sticky hands off her ass, I thought she'd be perfect for The Game. I'd figured Leo and I would have some fun with her, then buy her a bus ticket and send her on her way, someplace far from Vegas. We'd done it before. It was our *thing*.

But something was different this time.

I dropped the blue Tiffany box into my breast pocket and headed back to the office. Leo and I had business to tend to, and it wasn't going to be pleasant.

CHAPTER 20

LUCA

"Thanks for inviting us over, guys," my brother said, leaning back on a crackly leather sofa.

I looked at the four men in front of us, all clean-cut and unassuming. But appearances could be deceiving. These guys were some of the best card counters Vegas had ever seen.

I had to hand it to them. Card counting was hard shit. While you're not actually memorizing specific cards, you're assigning them a point score and keeping a running tally to assess the probability of whether you, or the dealer, has the advantage. If you get really good at counting, which very few people do, you can win a lot of fucking money by betting more but with less risk.

Hey, everybody wanted to win, right?

Problem was, we considered card counting an *unfair advantage*. And we didn't let unfair advantages happen on our dime.

"How many people do you have counting?" I asked.

One of them sat back in his chair and chuckled. "Like we're gonna fucking tell you that."

I shrugged. "It doesn't matter anyway. Our meeting today will send a message to the rest of your group."

The guy frowned back at me. "What the hell does that mean?"

"Look. We've warned you to stay away from our casinos. If you want to fuck with the others in town, that's for them to deal with. But we asked you to stay away, and since you haven't, you're going to pay the price."

The guy stood and started shouting. "Fuck you both. Get the hell out. I don't tell you how to run your business, and you don't tell me how to run mine."

I pointed a finger at him. "That's where you're wrong, my friend. *Your* business is costing *my* business money. Or I should say it *was*. Until today."

Leo and I headed for the door, leaving behind a litany of *fuck yous* and *go to hells*. As we exited, a couple of our guys entered the room. There was a bunch of shouting, and as we were about to exit the building, shots rang out.

The guys counting cards in our casinos? They wouldn't be doing it anymore.

I felt the Tiffany box in my pocket on the drive home. It was dangerous work we did, no doubt, and for some reason I couldn't shake the thought of what it would be like to not see Echo again.

You never knew when your last day on earth would be, and some lines of work further increased the likelihood of not making it home for dinner and ending up in the morgue, instead.

Funny, all the thinking I'd been doing about Echo.

I was usually a *one fuck* kind of guy, as Leo put it. Yup, I'd do a girl all night and send her home the next morning, never to be seen again. It was how I rolled. It had worked for years. I was a hard-hearted bastard.

I had a good reason to be.

It wasn't enough that our dad disappeared, when Leo and I were teenagers. A few years after that, our mother was murdered coming out of her hairdresser's. That was a fucking punch to the gut. It was some kind of message, I was certain, that they'd killed her but spared us. I'd been angry about it since it happened, and probably always would be.

When it came to doing jobs like the one we had today? I felt nothing. No remorse, no compassion, no sympathy. That's why my thoughts about Echo had thrown me off.

What the fuck was happening?

Just another day at the office, but somehow different.

When I got home, I scanned the house looking for

signs of Echo. But before I could find her, Mary greeted me with uncharacteristic happiness.

"Mr. Borroni, I hope you had a wonderful day."

Um, yeah, if offing card counters could be considered wonderful, then it was a pretty fucking awesome.

"Hey, Mary. Dinner smells great."

I ran up the stairs two at a time and knocked on Echo's door. I couldn't wait to see her with my necklace on, preferably naked, and sucking my dick.

Well, that last part would have to wait until after dinner.

When she didn't answer, I turned her doorknob slowly and peeked inside. "Echo? You here?"

I looked around her room and then checked out the window to see if she was down by the pool. Not there.

I ran into Smitt in the hallway. "Hey, is Echo down in the gym?"

He shook his head. "No. I wanted to talk to you about that. We don't know where she is."

"Wait. She's gone? Again?"

Was he fucking kidding?

"Smitt, I thought you had a couple of your guys watching her."

He nodded. "Yeah, I did. They brought her home, but she must have gone out again."

I shook my head. "What do you mean they brought her home? They weren't supposed to do that."

He put his hands on his hips and tried not to smile.

"Apparently she saw them trailing her. When she was done with her shopping, she approached them and asked for a ride home."

Oh, for fuck's sake.

"When you're trailing someone, Smitt, you're supposed to be *discreet*."

"Yup," he said.

I took a deep breath. "Is anyone looking for her?"

He shook his head. "Not at the moment."

I was trying not to explode. "You know I put that tracker in her phone the other night. Go find her for fuck's sake!"

Smitt raised his hand. "Okay, Luca, I know you're upset. I'm sorry. But you don't need to speak to me that way. We've been together a long time. You can crap on the other employees all you want, but not me."

He was right. I didn't like it, but he was right. Smitt was one of the few people in the world I knew could rely on.

"Luca," Smitt said, lowering his voice, "you can't expect to cage women. It's a kink that just doesn't work, at least not for very long. You know that."

It would be different with Echo. I knew it would.

"Would you go find her? Please?" I asked.

He nodded and headed for the door. "I'm on it. Are you still gonna play The Game with her?"

"I don't know. I haven't decided."

"Well. Leo said you—"

I stopped him. "I don't want to hear what Leo said."

I headed down the stairs to the gym. I needed to pound the shit out of my punching bag before I pounded the shit out of some human.

CHAPTER 21

ECHO

"Oh. My. God. This is beautiful. Where the hell did you get it?" Yasmina asked, looking at the cashmere sweater I'd brought her out of my own new stash. "This is from fucking *Saks*? I've never even had the balls to walk in there. So luxurious. Thank you, Echo."

"You're welcome. And the guy who's hosting me paid for it all. He just filled up this crazy big closet for me."

Hosting me. Funny way to put it.

Yasmina sat back on her barstool and looked at me skeptically. "What is this, a *Pretty Woman* revival?"

I play-slapped her hand. It had been only a few days, but god I'd missed her. The late-night talks we'd have, lying in one or the other's bed, just weren't the same over the phone.

"No, this is not *Pretty Woman*. Although we did have great sex." Tingles shot down my spine when I recalled the night before.

Yasmina squealed so loudly that everyone in the bar looked in our direction.

"Oops, loud," she said, without a hint of apology.

I leaned closer. "Maybe it's not like *Pretty Woman*. But it *is* like a romance novel. One of those down-and-dirty ones."

She waved her hands frantically. "Okay. Start at the beginning. Who is this guy, and how did you meet him?"

Shit. Of course she was going to want to know that.

"Well, um, I met these two brothers at Loaded Dice before, you know. Before everything happened." Best to keep it a little vague.

She was so excited, she was squirming in her seat. "Well, what are their names?"

"Luca and Leo Borroni. They're identical twins."

The smile slid off her face. "What did you just say? What were their names?" She took a gulp of her drink.

"Borroni. They're brothers, Luca and Leo—"

She spat whatever pink concoction she'd been drinking all over the bar and started coughing.

I jumped up to slap her back. "Oh my god, are you okay? Did you swallow wrong?"

She reached around and grabbed my hand.

"Are. You. Fucking. Crazy?" she asked, still sputtering.

"Huh? What do you mean?"

She put her hands on my shoulders and squeezed. "Haven't you been in Vegas long enough to know who to stay away from? The Borronis are the biggest mob family in town. Tell me you're hanging out with some *other* Borronis, and not the brothers. The *twin* brothers."

All I could do was stare at her, and then I got my voice back. "They've been very nice to me," I said in a small voice.

"Okay, Echo. This is no fucking romance novel. This is some dangerous shit. You can't get involved with these people."

Kind of late for that.

She arched her neck to stare at the ceiling. When she was done, she got right in my face. "Promise me you'll be careful. Call me if you need *anything*. I will be there to help you." She made me pinkie swear.

Much as I hated it, my eyes were welling with tears. I'd never had a friend like her—aside from my sister, Dini—someone who had my back unconditionally. It was new to have someone looking out for me. Or someone who cared enough about me to even *want* to look out for me.

"Hey," a male voice behind us said.

Yasmina and I turned from the bar and then looked back at each other.

We wore the same expression: *Do you know this guy? Because I don't.*

"Um, hi?" she said as a question.

A skinny blond guy beamed at us, gesturing nervously. "Hey. My friends and I over there were just talking about how pretty you two ladies were, and we thought we'd invite you to our table for a drink."

He pointed to his two friends, who were equally as clean-cut and preppy.

Yasmina jumped into what I called *Yas mode*.

She pursed her lips as she considered his offer, looking first from him, over to his friends, and back. Then, she stepped down off her barstool and sidled up to the guy until her lips were inches from his ear.

Poor bastard. He'd never know what hit him.

"What's your name?" she purred.

"Um… Scott. My name's Scott," he sputtered.

She accidentally-on-purpose rubbed her boobs against his arm. His friends, over at their table, guffawed and elbowed each other.

How old were these guys? Fifteen?

"Well, Scott, I have to ask you a question about your offer."

Oh no she didn't.

Yup, she ran her hand right over his package.

That's my Yasmina.

But Scott didn't know what to make of her and laughed nervously. He tried to twist out of her reach, but she held him firm.

He clearly thought he could keep up with her. "You're a sly one, aren't you?"

But there was no way he was a match for her. No one could keep up with Yasmina when she was on a tear.

She was like a black widow—she mated, then she killed.

She picked up his left hand and pointed to the wedding ring he'd forgotten to remove. "What I was gonna ask you, Scott, was whether your wife knows you're chatting up pretty girls in Las Vegas bars? I guess not, because she's probably having her own girls' night out right now. In fact, I bet she's sizing up which guy's dick she'll suck before the evening is over. All her friends will egg her on, and they'll laugh about it for years to come. And never mention a word of it to you."

God, she was evil. Good evil. Her wound inflected, she released the guy's crotch.

Scott snapped his head back, confused. Yup, he'd been thrown a curve ball of epic proportion. "You're crazy, you know that? My wife would never suck… she'd never do that." He started backing up and his friends, not having heard Yasmina's quiet speech, continued to beam.

Yasmina jumped back onto her barstool. "Now, he's gonna be wondering all weekend long what his wife is up to. He'll probably call and text her every five minutes."

She waved over the bartender for another round.

I was shaking so hard with laughter, it was a minute before I could speak. "You are a national treasure, Yas.

That's all I can say. I always pity the man who fucks with you."

Not one minute had gone by when we heard a ruckus behind us. We turned to find a commotion at the table Scott and his buds were occupying. Two huge guys were roughing them up.

Oh, shit.

They were the same guys who'd followed me in the mall that morning.

The guys who worked for Luca.

And who'd very nicely given me a lift home from the mall.

I jumped down off my barstool, and approached them. "Guys. *Guys*," I said louder, when I realized they were deep into it.

"Hey, Echo. Were these three bothering you?"

I felt sorry for the little prepsters.

"Not at all. My friend Yasmina was chatting one of them up."

The three guys stood, threw some money on their table, and hustled to the door, leaving their nearly full beers behind.

"They're gone now," I said as we watched them move like their asses were on fire.

"Echo, sorry to ruin the party, but we're supposed to bring you home."

Which home? Luca's home? Or my real home with Yasmina?

But I wasn't going to argue. Not then and not there.

"Okay, no problem. Come meet Yasmina while I take one more sip of my drink."

As I suspected, Yasmina got on with the security guys like a house on fire. Before I knew it, she'd ordered them a couple beers and we were all chatting.

Well, Yasmina was doing the chatting. She loved an audience. Which was why we were such good friends. I let her do the talking.

She regaled them with the terror she'd just inflicted on poor Scott, and they were nearly rolling on the floor, laughing.

One of them grabbed his vibrating phone. "Oh, shit. We gotta go. Smitt just texted. Luca is waiting for you."

"Oh god. You're going over *there*," Yasmina teased. "I hope you get some more dick tonight."

I slapped her arm. "Shut up, will you?"

She looked at her hunky new friends, and they all smiled knowingly. "Hey, guys, can I hitch a ride home?"

Just before we dropped Yasmina, she made sure to exchange contact information with the guys. All three of them *tap-tapped* on their phone screens until they were satisfied they were connected for life.

I got out of the car and hugged my girl. "Love you, Yas. We'll talk tomorrow, okay?"

She started skipping up the sidewalk to our apartment. "Yeah," she called, "you need to come by the shop. Your hair's starting to look like shit."

I shook my head, laughing, and thanked god she was on my team.

CHAPTER 22

ECHO

"Hi, GUYS," I said as soon as I'd walked into the twins' house.

Weird. They were just standing there waiting for me.

I looked back when the door slammed behind me, but the security guards must not have followed me in.

I didn't get to thank them.

"What the fuck were you doing?" Leo asked, taking a step toward me.

"Um, what?" I asked.

He hardly ever spoke to me.

"Was I supposed to ask permission before leaving the house? Because if that's how you want to run this, that's bullshit and won't work for me at all." I rolled my eyes at them both and started for the stairs.

"Come back here," Luca growled.

Seriously?

I felt like a high schooler in trouble for having sneaked a smoke in the bathroom.

"What?" I snapped.

"You broke the rules."

I sighed in frustration. "What rules? How can there be rules when you've never shared *a single one of them* with me?" I was getting shrill.

"C'mon," Luca said, grabbing me by the arm.

I tried to pull away. "Where are we going? What the hell is going on?"

We headed toward the library, or should I say, the guys headed for the library and dragged me along. Leo pushed open the doors and locked them once we were inside.

"There are consequences for breaking rules," Luca said, matter-of-factly.

I shrugged. "Okay. If you say so. I don't know what the rules are, but if you say I broke them, fine. I'm sorry," I said with a deep bow.

"Are you fine?" Leo asked.

"Look, I don't know what kind of bullshit you guys are up to, but I'm tired and am going to bed."

I headed for the library's door, but Leo stopped me.

"Go over to Luca," he barked.

"Really, guys? Seriously, I'm tired. I was out for a drink with Yasmina. What's the big deal?" But I walked over to Luca anyway. The sooner I figured out what the hell they wanted, the sooner I could go to sleep.

Luca was perched on the edge of a leather ottoman. "Here," he said, reaching for my hand.

In one swift movement, he had me bent over his lap with my ass in the air.

"What the fuck?" I screamed. "Let me up. I'm not in the mood to mess around. I told you, I'm *tired*."

"This isn't *messing around*," Luca said, reaching under me to open the fly of my jeans.

"Leo, can you please help me? Talk some sense into your brother?" I craned my neck to see where he was and found him looking very comfortable in an oversized easy chair.

With a clear view of my ass.

Which was now naked, Luca having slid my jeans and thong panty down to my knees.

I squirmed in embarrassment. Sure, Luca had seen me naked, but I wasn't thrilled about baring it for Leo, too.

"Let me up," I screamed, pounding on Luca's legs, the only things within my reach.

Smack.

"Ouch!" I hollered when his open palm landed on my ass.

Smack.

"Stop it, Luca. I swear, this is not funny."

Smack.

There was a slight groan behind me, and I realized Leo was enjoying the show.

I hoped he was also enjoying my spread-open pussy, too, because he sure was getting an eyeful. I would have liked to crawl away in shame, but that was obviously out of the question with Luca's arm holding me down like a vise.

Smack. Smack. Smack.

After a while, I could only grunt when one of Luca's blows landed on my burning flesh. And the funny thing was, I could swear I was getting wet from the spanking, a fact that was verified when he dipped his fingers into my pussy lips.

"Look how turned on she is," he said to his brother.

When he finally stopped spanking me, I couldn't move. I was stiff from being bent over his lap, and my ass cheeks were burning so badly I was afraid to move.

But the guys didn't care.

"You can get up now," Luca said.

Leo walked over and taking my arm, helped me stand.

Unfortunately, my legs weren't ready, and they buckled under me.

"Here we go, baby," Luca said, suddenly all sweet. He pulled my jeans up to cover me, scooped me into his arms, and headed for my room.

"Good night, beautiful," Leo called after me.

I was millimeters from giving him the finger, but I couldn't deal with any more bullshit for one night.

Luca laid me on my bed and pulled off my boots. He kissed my temple and turned to leave.

When he reached the door, he turned for one last look. "This will be locked from the outside until you learn to follow the rules. If you need anything, knock and we'll come." He pulled the door closed.

Was he fucking kidding me?

I pushed myself up in bed and gingerly removed the panties and jeans stuck to my sweaty flesh. I waddled to the door as best I could and found he hadn't lied.

I was indeed locked inside my fucking bedroom.

I yanked on the doorknob several times as if it might magically come loose, and then I pounded.

"You can't do this," I screamed. "I am not your prisoner, you motherfuckers. Wait 'til I get out of here."

It was looking less and less likely that I was going to be escaping my 'obligation,' as Luca called it. Also known as The Game.

I needed a plan B, if I was going to survive three months in this shitshow.

Hours later, a ringing doorbell jolted me awake. It must have been ungodly early, because my room was still mostly dark. Had something new been delivered for me?

Christ, these guys had me trained like freaking Pavlov's dog.

But on the other hand, I probably wasn't eligible for presents when I'd been a bad girl.

I pulled my cashmere robe on—yes, they'd gotten

me a *cashmere* robe—and tiptoed over to the door, where I pressed my ear to it.

I recognized Luca and Leo's voices, but there was a third man speaking, whose voice I did not recognize.

"Is the girl still here?" the stranger asked.

Shit. Was I *the girl*? And why did this person want to know my whereabouts?

After that, all I could hear were muffled voices. But, to be honest, I'd heard enough to have the shit scared out of me.

I looked around my room in a panic. The windows were too high off the ground to make an escape, and there were really no other options.

Until I remembered the attic door.

I ran into my closet, the pain from my spanking temporarily forgotten, and placed a chair directly under the rope that hung from the ceiling. With a small tug, a folding staircase opened that reached all the way to the floor.

Before I climbed them, I grabbed my phone and turned on the flashlight app.

I inched my way up the narrow steps, and when I was far enough up to see in, I shined the light into the darkness.

Hmmm.

I wasn't sure whether to be disappointed or relieved. Maybe both?

The room was just an unfinished attic filled with leftover building supplies. Nothing sinister or even interesting. But I *was* happy I'd found a potential hiding place.

I crawled into a corner of the mostly-empty room, drawing my knees to my chest and wrapping my arms around them. Then I closed my eyes, pretending everything was fine.

CHAPTER 23

LUCA

Sal had woken us all up out of a dead sleep. I wasn't happy about it.

"I told you, everything's under control, Sal."

I wasn't inviting him any further into the house. He may have been a second father to Leo and me, but that didn't mean he could get into every bit of our business, particularly when it came to Echo. We could have our conversation in the foyer, and hopefully he'd get the message that we weren't up for 'visitors.'

And then get the hell out of our house. It was the goddamn ass-crack of dawn.

Leo put his hands on his hips. "I don't understand what the problem is, Sal."

He took a deep breath, as if he were losing patience.

"I've told you guys already. I think she knows too much. The girl knows too much."

Leo shook his head. "That's bullshit. She doesn't know anything."

Sal waved his hands impatiently. "She knows you took out her boss and the rest of the people at Loaded Dice. All she needs to do is share that gory story with the wrong people and we are fucked. I'm not worried about the police getting word—I'm concerned about the rest of the syndicate finding out. They can't be trusted, and personally, I'd like to live a little longer. So get her a bus ticket, give her a wad of cash, and send her away before she shoots her mouth off."

No. Absolutely not. I had plans for Echo. *We* had plans for Echo.

Not that Sal needed to know that.

We'd always deferred to him. He was used to it, and so were we. Shit, when our dad disappeared, Leo and I had already been working in the family business for a few years, although not doing any heavy lifting to speak of. Sal had taught us everything our dad would have, because someday he'd no longer be around and we'd be running the show. He wanted us prepared.

He pointed his finger at Leo and then me. "I've told you what needs to be done." He turned on his heel, slamming the door behind himself.

"Well, we really pissed him off this time," Leo said with his usual smirk.

I didn't care. "I'm not willing to comply. What about you?"

Leo shook his head. "Fuck him. I hate to say this about someone who's been so good to us, but he's losing touch. Times are changing, and he's not getting with the program."

Mary stuck her head into the foyer. "Would you gentlemen like some breakfast?"

Leo and I both said *no.*

"But you might make some for Echo. She probably will."

Mary scowled and walked back to the kitchen without a word.

I went down to the gym for my workout. I was desperate for some time on the punching bag to blow off steam. First, I was annoyed that Sal was getting involved in my personal business. He had no say in who we kept at our house, and he had to learn to trust us in that regard.

Second, I was mad at myself for reacting to Echo the way I had the night before. So what if she'd gone out for a drink with her girlfriend. It was completely innocent. She hadn't been trying to vex us.

But Leo and I had our rules, and we stuck to them. It was the only way things could operate.

As I began working up a good sweat, my thoughts turned to how I still didn't know much about her.

Yet.

Why was she responsible for her sister?

Where was she from?

Did she have any other family?

I wanted to know it all.

And I couldn't understand what drove me to enter her room at night just to watch her breathe.

Why did my heart break a little when I walked past her door after spanking her and I heard her crying? I wanted to go in and comfort her, lie with her, hold her, and wake up with her.

But that wasn't how Leo and I operated.

I rubbed a towel over my sweaty face and climbed the stairs, two at a time. I had to see her and couldn't wait any longer.

"Echo?" I said, knocking on her door.

When there was no answer, I got a burning sensation in my stomach.

Where the fuck was she?

I burst into her room. "Echo?" I hollered.

Goddamnit.

"Yo, why are you yelling?" Leo asked, sticking his head in her room.

My head was beginning to pound. "She's fucking gone again."

Leo walked in, looking around the room as if in approval. "Well, she kept the place tidy." He pulled open the closet doors and found all the clothes we'd given her still there.

"You know, Luc," he said, "if you hadn't been so hard on her, maybe she wouldn't have run off. She's probably gone for good this time." He shrugged like he didn't give a shit.

Was he fucking kidding?

"Well, bro, I didn't see you protesting when we were punishing her. You sat there looking at her ass in the air, licking your chops."

"Whatever. How are we going to get The Game going, if you keep driving her off?"

I clenched my fists at my sides so I didn't hit him.

"Guys, guys, let's take it down a notch."

We both turned to see Smitt.

"She's missing again?" he asked. "Christ, she's wily."

I glared. "How the hell did she get out?"

"It's not that hard. But don't worry. I know where to look."

CHAPTER 24

ECHO

"Here's another duffel. Put some of your stuff in here," Yasmina said, unzipping a tattered old nylon bag on my twin bed in the apartment we shared.

I grabbed it from her and stuffed the rest of my things inside, not that I had all that much to begin with. I could have taken some of the nice things Luca and Leo had gotten me from my room there, but I didn't feel right about it.

Imagine that, having a conscience about ripping off guys who were essentially in the mob and were holding me prisoner. The irony.

I ran into the bathroom to gather up my things there, which didn't amount to much more than Covergirl lip gloss, some cheap nail polish, and a hair dryer from the drugstore.

Actually, I put the nail polish back in the medicine cabinet. I didn't need that shit.

"What else can I help with?" Yasmina asked.

I looked around our apartment, exquisitely sad about saying goodbye to it—and her.

I shrugged. "I think I've got everything. You can have my plants. And here. I'm giving you two months' rent to tide you over until you get a new roomie."

I'd miss that dream bedroom at Luca and Leo's. I couldn't lie. And I really might have enjoyed the hidden attic room, where—I still couldn't believe my luck—I'd found a key.

A key that opened my bedroom door from the inside.

I needed to thank *someone* for that. I just didn't know *who*. Previous tenant, maybe?

"I don't want a new roomie." Yasmina bit her bottom lip, and her eyes got shiny.

"No crying. Because if you start, I will, too."

She sniffled and shook her head to chase off the tears. "I'll miss you. But we'll meet up again. Somehow."

I threw my arms around her so tight I probably hurt her. God, I hoped I'd see her again. I'd never had a friend like Yasmina. So kick-ass, gutsy, fucking hilarious, and loyal to a fault. She had my back at all times. I hadn't had anyone like that in my life since my grandmother passed, and I was going to miss her terribly, just like I did my gran.

"Let me check my room one last time."

So Yasmina wouldn't see my tears, I escaped to the simple little room I was abandoning, furnished with a bed, nightstand, lamp, and a small IKEA dresser. Some tenant from long ago had left these things behind, and the landlord, knowing how transient Vegas was and how many people came here broke with the hopes of making their fortune, left it all there for the next person.

And the next.

It wasn't much, but when I'd moved in, I was beyond thrilled. I'd never had a room of my own, having always shared with my sister.

Don't get me wrong—I never minded sharing with Dini. But there was something so luxurious about having a room all to myself, I almost felt guilty. It seemed so indulgent and over-the-top, especially for someone like me who didn't have two nickels to rub together.

Actually, that was a bit of an exaggeration. I had more than two nickels to rub together when I arrived in Vegas. There was five hundred dollars in my pocket when I'd left West Virginia. I'd never had that kind of money before, and it felt damn good, even if the way I came to acquire it, didn't.

When I was ten and Dini seven, our dad was killed working as a security guard. It had been fucking devastating on so many levels, and as if that weren't bad enough, my sister was diagnosed with muscular dystrophy after a lifetime of being labeled a 'klutzy kid.' She was in a wheelchair within the year. As soon as she could, our mother shipped us off to our grandmother's, claiming she was too bereft to care for two little girls.

Although, she'd never been that interested in us anyway. I'd always suspected she'd had us kids just to keep my dad—and his paycheck—around.

Being shipped off to Gran's turned out to be a good move for everyone involved.

Our dad's mom, Gran, was kind and loving just like our father had been, and while we didn't have much, we always had what we needed. We saw little of our mother during those years, which came to an abrupt end when I was a senior in high school and Dini was fourteen. Life decided to throw us another shit-covered curve ball.

Some people had all the luck.

I'd come home from school and found Gran dead, which I later learned was the result of a heart attack. While it was beyond horrible, I was just happy it had been me and not Dini who found her.

What really devastated me was that I hadn't gotten to say goodbye—just like I hadn't with my dad. The day he was killed, he'd been eating his usual buttered toast, standing at the kitchen sink. Before he left, he took one more gulp of his coffee and said over his shoulder while running out the door, "See ya later, pretty ladies."

Dini and I looked at each other and smiled. He was always full of compliments like that. But that was the last one we got from him, because he never came home.

And now Gran was gone.

This time, Mom stepped up to the plate, if only in her half-assed sort of way. She insisted on taking Dini in. After all, she was still in high school and in a wheelchair.

But she didn't want me. So I finished out the school year living alone in Gran's house. One evening, when cleaning out some of her things, I came across a small tea tin that I almost threw out. But something told me to open it, and inside was five hundred dollars.

I'd never seen a one-hundred-dollar bill, let alone five of them.

It was all the money Gran had in the world, and now it was mine. I wasn't sure it was *supposed* to be mine, but I was sure as hell helping myself to it.

Gran's cash got me to Vegas and sustained me until I landed a minimum-wage job at a pawnshop dealing with the dregs of Las Vegas humanity, which eventually led me to Loaded Dice, where I got an even bigger taste of Las Vegas humanity.

And that job sure had worked out well.

A hand on my shoulder scared the shit out of me. "C'mon. We gotta go. You have to get out of here before anyone notices you're gone," Yasmina said, pretending not to see the tears on my cheeks.

We hoisted the duffels over our shoulders and hustled out to her car. Once in the passenger seat, I put on sunglasses and sank as low as I could for the ride to the bus station.

As if that would fool anyone.

"Christ, I hope this works, Echo," Yasmina said, pulling into traffic.

"I don't know why it wouldn't—" I started to say, just as there was a little *bump* against her car.

"What the fuck!" She looked around frantically, adjusting her rearview mirror to figure out what had happened.

Bump.

Shit. It had happened again.

"What's going on, Yas?" I asked, popping up in my seat to look around.

"I don't know," she cried, "but whoever hit us is now trying to pass us on my side."

"Maybe they want to give us their insurance information?"

She gripped the steering wheel with white knuckles and looked out her side window nervously. "I don't think so. Look how close they're driving to us!"

She rolled down her window. "Fuck off, asshole," she screamed.

That was how Yasmina dealt with problems.

But her saltiness had no impact this time.

The car just got closer.

And closer.

Until they scraped against us again.

I screamed, and Yasmina struggled to keep the car straight.

All the other cars on the freeway looked on in horror and gave us a wide berth. I didn't understand why no one was helping us.

But on the other hand, what the fuck could they do?

With one last sideswipe, Yasmina's car was pushed to the shoulder of the road, where the front right side of the car—where I was sitting—skidded into the guardrail.

She had no choice but to stop.

"What's going on? Why would someone do this?" she wailed as the car doors were pulled open by some big guys I'd never seen before.

But I knew what was going on, and why someone would run us off the road.

I even knew who was behind it.

"Oh my god, Echo. You guys get off her," Yasmina screamed. In all her fierceness, she'd crawled over me and began beating their arms, trying to pull me back into her car.

It had done no good.

"You can't do this, you fuckers," she'd screamed as two guys threw me in the back seat of their SUV and drove away.

CHAPTER 25

ECHO

"WHO THE FUCK do you think you are?" I demanded, barging into Luca's office after having brushed aside his secretary.

I didn't give a fuck about her or their office decorum. Yasmina and I could have been killed by the henchmen who'd run us off the road. I'd been so screaming mad when they stuffed me in their car, I think they were all too happy to get rid of me at Luca's building.

And now I was looking at his beautiful goddamn face, wearing a small smile that I wanted to smack into next week. I clenched my fists so hard my nails cut my palms. I hated him more than I'd ever hated anyone.

Deep breath, girl. Deep breath.

Without breaking his gaze, which was locked with

mine, he waved a hand at the others in his office. "Would you gentlemen please excuse my friend Echo and me?"

They hustled out, but not before Leo winked at me. Jerk.

"I'm not your goddamn friend, you asshole," I spat when the last person was gone.

He considered what I'd said. "I can see why you'd say that."

"Your fucking henchmen could have killed Yasmina and me."

"But they didn't. And here you are, safe. *Again.*"

"Fuck you, Luca. I'd be a lot safer if you'd leave me the hell alone."

He got up and walked around his desk, looking so goddamn sexy, I hated him even more.

And there I was, wearing the shitty old clothes I'd owned *pre-Luca,* my hair a mess and not a stitch of makeup on my face.

His colleagues had probably thought me some sort of nasty Vegas guttersnipe. But that was okay. Because —*fuck them,* too.

"You don't understand what's going on here," he said.

"Oh, I understand. You think I'm your prisoner. You think you did me some big favor by making sure I didn't get killed in the Loaded Dice shootout. Well, you didn't. I'd rather you had shot me too, just like you did my boss and everyone else."

It was almost imperceptible, but his face twitched. Before he could recover, I would swear a hint of sadness passed over his eyes.

"I never would have done that. I could never hurt you."

I threw my arms up in the air. "What? You think keeping me a prisoner isn't hurting me?" I wailed.

He was silent.

And there we had it. It hadn't crossed his crime-addled mind that I didn't want to be his fucking Rapunzel.

He took a step toward me and put his hands on my shoulders. Before I could shrug him off, I had a revelation.

But maybe it *had* crossed his mind.

And he just didn't care.

"Listen to me, Echo," he said in a quiet voice. "I want you to be happy—or as happy as you possibly can be. But I won't beg you to stay. If you hate… *this*… so much, or hate *me* so much, I'll let you walk. I won't like it, but I'll let you walk."

Stunned, I felt a damn lump growing in my throat for the second time that day.

He'd listened.

Which was all I really wanted.

"But if you agree to stay, I need to protect you. There are people out there who will try to hurt you to get to me."

"Who?" I asked quietly.

He shrugged. "Any number of people. The Borroni family has enemies. We always have. They are undoubtedly responsible for the disappearance of my father and murder of my mother. You have to stop running away. I will always find you."

He ran his fingertips down my arm until he reached my hand.

"I've wanted you since the first time I saw you serving drinks."

"Why? You could have any woman you wanted," I said.

He ran the fingertips of his other hand over my cheek, and damn if he didn't have me quivering in my Chucks.

I leaned on a chair just to steady myself.

"I don't have an answer for that," he whispered and lowered his mouth to mine.

His lips were softer—more tender—than the last time he'd kissed me. There was no sense of urgency, but rather a play for reconciliation. I might have been imagining it, but I was pretty sure he was trying to persuade me back to his side of the aisle.

And of course, I returned his kiss, our mouths opening as our connection deepened. He smelled so good—just clean guy, which made me want him even more.

There was something about a natural man that just about killed me.

He propped me on the edge of his desk and went to

his office door, locking it. He pulled the blinds down on the windows facing the hallways. I knew what was coming.

And I couldn't wait.

Which pissed me the fuck off. Damn him.

He strolled toward me, opening his tie the way guys do when they pull them off over their heads. He threw his suit jacket on the back of a chair and began to unbutton the cuffs of his expensive white dress shirt, his fingers crunching over the starchy cotton.

The whole time, watching me.

With his shirt tossed aside, he bent to remove his shoes and socks.

Holy fucking shit.

He reached for his belt and fly and in a swift movement, let his pants and boxers fall to the floor.

There he stood before me, broad shoulders and defined pecs narrowing to a slim waist, which led to a beautiful, hard cock.

I couldn't tear my eyes away.

I'd seen Luca naked before. I mean, I'd fucked him only a couple nights ago. But I'd not seen him standing in all his glory like he was just then.

And it was amazing.

He gestured at me with his chin. "Take off your clothes."

"I... I..."

I couldn't move. I couldn't even spit out any words.

"Take them off, I said," he repeated.

With clumsy fingers, I lifted my T-shirt over my head and unbuttoned my jeans. I kicked off my sneakers and socks and tossed them into Luca's pile.

All I had left to remove were my thong panties and bra.

"You know how fucking beautiful you are, Echo?"

I slowly shook my head.

"Then I'll teach you," he said, walking toward me.

With hands on either side of my face, he studied me like an inanimate object. As if he'd never seen a woman's face up close before and he wanted to memorize every angle and plane.

Then his hands slipped to my shoulders. In one swift movement, he spun me to face the desk and bent me over, leaving me folded at a right angle.

I twisted to see what he was doing, but he pushed my head down until my cheek pressed into a pile of papers on his desk. It was not comfortable.

He slid my thong to just below my ass and rubbed his giant cock between my cheeks, which he had so mercilessly beaten only a couple nights before.

I tried to part my legs for him, but with my panties at my thighs, they were pretty much bound together.

Luca shifted behind me, his hands on my ass.

He spread my cheeks.

Oh god, he isn't going there.

But he was.

His tongue passed over my asshole, throwing me

into a tizzy of goose bumps. No one had ever done that. I didn't know whether to relax or be terrified.

But he pressed his tongue down there even harder, and damn if it didn't feel like heaven. My wet pussy dripped down my thigh, and I prayed he didn't see how excited I was.

"You like it, baby?" he murmured.

"Mmmm" was all I would say.

"Okay. Tell me to stop if you want."

Oh, cripes. A finger entered me very slowly and gently, and you know what?

It was fucking awesome.

As he probed deeper, his cock notched just at the opening of my pussy. I could move very little but pushed back against him.

"You ready, baby?" he asked.

"Yeah. Fuck me," I whispered.

He pushed his cock inside me to the hilt, and I shrieked. It was like some sort of explosion had gone off in my brain, and all I could see were bright lights and hear the rush of blood though my ears.

There was nothing else.

As he pumped my pussy, his finger drove in and out of my ass for the most unbelievable sensation I'd ever felt.

Every nerve in my body was firing. My arms and legs were shaking. My face ground into his desk, which I slammed my hand against over and over, creating a ruckus that surely alerted the rest of the office to what we were doing.

And I couldn't have cared less.

A growl rose in Luca's throat, and he drove into me so deeply one last time that his desk slipped on the floor beneath us.

"Fuck..." he groaned.

He collapsed, burrowing his hands under me to hold my shaking body. As soon as he caught his breath, he pushed aside my hair and ran his lips up and down the side of my neck.

Who knew sex could be like that? Not me, that was for damn sure. I'd really only been with the dumbass hicks in my small town, and it was all they could do to locate a vagina, never mind figure out what to do with one.

I'd almost forgotten how mad I was at Luca.

Almost.

CHAPTER 26

LUCA

PEELING the limp Echo off my desk, I settled her into one of my office chairs. I redressed her and then pulled on my shirt and trousers, not bothering with the tie. I'd seen a shadow or two pass under my office door, but my people knew better than to knock. If my blinds were closed, I was fucking *busy*.

Echo pushed herself to her feet, still wobbly.

"You okay, darlin'?" I asked, taking her elbow.

She looked down, nodding.

I lifted her chin to see her eyes. "The Game is for three months. We don't have a lot of rules, but the ones we have must be followed. You will be cared for and live well, but you will be controlled. I have to know you're on board with this. I would never force you."

No, I could never force a woman. Or even pressure one. But I did hope I could persuade Echo.

"I… I don't know. I mean, I need to get a job. My sister at home depends on me."

I shook my head. "You don't need to work. Everything will be taken care of. You will be paid, and paid very well. In fact, you will be set for life."

"Are you serious?" she asked, finally looking up at me.

I had to laugh at that. "You clearly don't know me very well. But you will. In time you'll trust me and know I mean what I say."

That was something she and I had in common. I didn't trust people, and neither did she. When your dad disappears one day, and not long after that your mom is murdered, you go through the rest of your life looking over your shoulder, always wondering if you're next.

The good news was, however, that when you did find someone you could trust, it felt fucking awesome.

Like Echo.

But she didn't trust me—yet. And I couldn't blame her. I wanted to get to the bottom of her story and teach her she could trust some people, namely me.

"C'mon. Let's go home," I said, extending my hand.

She didn't take it.

Which was fine. She wasn't ready. But she would be soon.

Once in my Tesla, she turned to me. "All my stuff is

still in Yasmina's car. Your guys scared the shit out of both of us."

That was kind of the point.

I steered out of our secure parking garage. "Maybe you could have her over sometime. Hang out at the pool and have Mary make you lunch."

I glanced over to see her features soften.

"Have Mary make lunch for Yas and me? She'd probably poison us." Her head dropped back, and she laughed, her eyes closed.

I surprised myself with a visceral feeling, but realized that if anyone ever touched Echo, I'd kill them. With my bare hands if I had to.

Jesus. Relax, guy.

"I'll send someone to get your stuff, if you want it."

She shrugged. "Eh. Not sure I do. It's just a bunch of junk. Nothing I really need. I just felt like I should take it out of Yas's apartment so she could let someone else move in."

"How much is your rent there?" I asked.

She looked out the window as we passed ugly strip mall after ugly strip mall. I loved Vegas, had lived there all my life, but its ugly parts were serious eyesores.

"Four hundred fifty a month. Yas pays a little more since she has the bigger room."

Easy solution.

"Tell ya what. Let me pay your rent for six months in advance so your friend doesn't have to worry about getting a new roommate yet."

She looked at me, and I could see she was doing math in her head, wondering why I offered beyond her three month obligation to Leo and me. "Well, maybe."

Echo's phone rang and she swiped it open.

She lowered her voice and turned toward the window for privacy. "Sissy."

A heard a perky female voice on the other end of the line.

"I'm glad school is good, sweetie. Were the groceries I ordered delivered?"

She nodded. "Has Mom been around?" she asked and a moment later, put her head in her hand.

"Dini, you know you can come out here tomorrow if you want. I've saved a bit of money, and you can have it for the trip."

Christ. This woman really had some serious grown-up shit going on.

"All right. I'll call you tomorrow. Love you."

When we got home, we took seats at the kitchen counter after I'd sent Mary home. I wasn't in the mood for her drama, and she left dinner in the oven.

I'd talked Echo into having a glass of wine, and poured soda water for myself.

"So what's the deal with your sister?"

She took a deep breath and played with the stem of her wineglass. "Basically, our grandma raised us after our dad died. Our mom couldn't deal. Or didn't want to, I should say. Then, when Gran died, Mom took Dini back in. But our Mom's a drunk and disappears for days at a time."

"You're kidding."

Christ.

"So I've been trying to get Dini to come out here. But it's sounding more and more like she's afraid to leave Mom. She has some sense of responsibility or loyalty toward her, which baffles me. Our Mom was never there for us, and with Dini in a wheelchair, she's less than useless, if that's even possible."

I put my hand over Echo's. "What can I do to help?"

Her gaze met mine. "I'm not sure. But thank you for asking. Thank you so much."

"I'll tell you what. Why don't you go get cleaned up and we'll go to a nice dinner tonight. I can put all the stuff Mary made in the fridge for another time."

She shrugged, still not sure about me. "I guess we could do that. But won't Mary get mad?"

I laughed. "Probably. But I don't care. Let's leave in an hour."

I had some calls to make to pull the evening together and patted my breast pocket where Echo's Tiffany gift still sat.

My girl was going to be blown away.

I set things up with a couple phone calls and jogged up to my room to freshen up.

CHAPTER 27

LUCA

I CHECKED my phone as soon as I'd gotten out of the shower and found a text message from Sal.

did you get rid of her yet?

Fucking asshole.

I loved the man, but there was just no seeing eye to eye on this.

When I didn't answer him, he tried again.

we cannot let any attachments or distractions impact our work, luca. you know that.

I let that sit for a moment while I dressed in dark blue jeans, another starched white dress shirt, and a navy blazer.

you needn't worry. our focus is impeccable. just like it's always been.

I wanted to add *get over it old man*. But I refrained. I had more important things on my mind.

Returning to the kitchen, I opened another water and waited for Echo. And not a moment too soon, she made her entrance.

And what an entrance it was.

She'd apparently rummaged through all the clothing my team had brought her and pulled together something so hot, so perfect, and so *her* that my dick began to immediately twitch.

And she knew she looked fucking good.

She walked across the kitchen toward me, her gaze locked on mine. Skinny leather jeans hugged her curvy hips like they were painted on her, and a loose silver top hung over her tits, sparkling as her bare breasts swung underneath it.

Her heels, which I knew were by Jimmy Choo because I'd personally selected them, must have been five inches high. But she walked in them perfectly, and she stopped right in front of me, pulling on a tailored black blazer to complete her outfit.

Fucking A.

"Goddamn, baby," I said, pulling her to me for a soft kiss.

She smiled shyly. I liked that. A beautiful but modest woman.

"I have something for you." I pulled the Tiffany box out of my pocket.

Her eyes widened as she took it. "Is this from Tiffany?"

"It is."

She pressed her lips together. "I'm not sure I'm comfortable accepting this."

I loved her directness, and grabbed the box back out of her hand.

"Okay," I said, tossing it to the end of the kitchen counter.

She stared where it sat, just out of her reach. "I've never been in Tiffany. Dini and I love the movie, though. You know, the one with Audrey Hepburn?"

I laughed. "Yeah. *Breakfast at Tiffany's*. It's a classic."

She couldn't take her eyes off it. "The blue is just so pretty."

Goddamn she was a sweetheart.

"Well, I think you should at least open it to see what's inside. Or I'll be upset."

She smirked at me mockingly. "And we know what you do when you're upset. My ass is still sore."

I gestured at the box. "C'mon."

She reached for it, pulling the top off, and gasped. Reaching inside, she pulled out the platinum key I'd chosen and dangled it by its chain.

She turned it over in her fingers. "Are these diamonds?" she asked breathlessly.

That's when I knew I'd made the right choice.

"They are."

She looked up at me, then back at the necklace. "I don't want to put it on, because then I can't see it."

Guess she'd decided she wanted it.

"But if you put it on, then *I* can see it," I said.

"That's true. It's just so beautiful. And a key is so symbolic."

I knew she'd *get it*.

"Thank you. Thank you so much," she whispered.

She turned so I could clasp it behind her neck. When she faced me, the platinum metal glowed against her skin, where it dangled just above her tits.

"You ready to go?" I asked.

She fingered the key. I had a feeling she'd be touching it all night.

"Seriously. I don't mind if we just stay in and eat what Mary prepared. This necklace is very generous."

Smitt walked into the room, always good about his timing. "You guys ready?"

Echo looked back at me. "Where are we going?"

"To LA," I said.

She frowned. "Um, that's about a five-hour drive. Isn't that kind of far for dinner?"

Smitt spoke up. "You're not driving to LA. You're flying. In a helicopter."

"*What?*"

"C'mon, guys, I gotta get you to the McCarran heliport so you don't miss your charter," Smitt said.

Echo's fingers flew back to her new key, as if it were a comfort.

165

CHAPTER 28

LUCA

WHEN WE ARRIVED at the heliport, a concierge directed us to our ride, a shiny black Robinson R44, and once we were in the air, Echo took a deep breath.

"I've never been in a helicopter. I've never even been in a plane."

I took her hand, and this time she didn't pull away. "Squeeze my fingers if you're afraid. But try and enjoy the view of the desert. It's really amazing, and the sun will be going down soon." Pulling her to me, I kissed her temple.

She didn't resist, and in fact pressed her hands against the window for a better view. "It's incredible, seeing everything from this perspective. My god."

"I thought you might like it."

"Where are we going to dinner?"

"To Urasawa. One of the best restaurants in LA, and it's very exclusive. Only ten seats."

Her eyes widened. "Are you serious? How'd you get a table there? And am I dressed okay?"

She was more than okay.

"I know the chef. We go way back."

The helicopter ride was over before we knew it, and I realized it felt good to be in LA. It had been a while, and there was something festive about the place. And it was always nice to get a break from the super-dry air in Vegas.

When we arrived at the restaurant, the chef came out and walked us to our table. "So good to see you, Luca," he said.

"You too, brother. This is my friend Echo."

She extended her hand. "Beautiful place. And, I've never had Japanese food."

"No way! Well, I'll be sure to send out only my best. I want to make sure you come back." He showed us to our seats, and poured Echo some of his best sake.

She took a look around. "Oh my god. I think that's Leonardo DiCaprio over there," she whispered.

I leaned toward her over the table and whispered back. "It probably is."

She began playing with her key again.

"This is incredible," she breathed, trying not to stare as Kate Hudson came in with her mother, Goldie Hawn.

"You're pretty incredible," I told her.

The thirty-course meal that Urasawa was famous for began coming out, and in moments, our table was covered in dishes.

The bright expression on Echo's face faded, to what I could swear was sadness.

"What is it?" I asked.

Surprise crossed her face. "I was just thinking how light-years away this is from West Virginia, and how my sister might never have such a special experience. I need to get her out of my mother's house." She waved her hand as if to dismiss something. "But let's talk about something fun. I don't want to ruin dinner with my preoccupations."

It was time.

"There is something I wanted to discuss with you."

She took a bite of red snapper nigiri and closed her eyes, moaning. "Wow. It's like butter melting in my mouth. It's not at all gross like I thought it would be."

I burst out laughing at that one. I couldn't help myself. She just said whatever the hell was on her mind.

"Leo and I wanted to let you know more about The Game."

"Oh. right. Is that a board game, or something online like Words With Friends?" she asked, laughing.

Better take this slow.

"Very funny."

Did I really want to go there? Was Echo right for The Game? And was I doing this just to satisfy Leo?

Why had I even brought it up?

I knew why. Because I *had* to. It was part of the plan.

And we didn't deviate from the plan.

"So The Game is something that can set you up for life, like I told you," I said.

She laughed again. "Oh, so it's like multilevel marketing or something? Do I have to sell Amway?" She piled a huge bite of grilled shiitake into her mouth.

"Funny girl."

I poured her some more sake.

"Seriously, what does *set up for life* mean?" She titled her head, all business.

I took a deep breath. "What do you think it means, Echo?"

She rolled her eyes.

"If you agree to participate, you are essentially mine and Leo's. I am your primary, meaning we can be together whenever we want, and Leo would be your secondary."

"Oh. It's sexual, then? Would I be some sort of prostitute?"

I knew that was coming. The other women who'd played The Game with us asked the same.

"You are not a prostitute. This is a game, which you will play if you want. Leo and I have a lot of... assets, and we are happy to share them with deserving people."

"Okay. And what does that mean, that Leo is secondary?"

I never knew how a woman would react when we invited her to The Game. Some reacted with repulsion, which let us know she wasn't right for us. Some were so excited they couldn't wait to get started.

And some were hard to read, like Echo.

"Leo can only be with you when I am there, watching. But he can also watch us. You and me."

Yeah, we were kinky fucks.

She gulped, and then almost imperceptibly, one corner of her mouth turned up. I was pretty sure I had her.

"Like a threesome?" she said quietly.

"Have you ever thought of something like that?" I asked.

Of course she had. Who hasn't thought about threesomes?

She gave me a nod. A very small nod. "Um, I've thought about it."

"Think you'd like it?" I asked.

This time, she shifted in her seat.

"Yes."

Perfect.

"What about the other girls?" she asked. "I'm sure there have been others."

Another question I was anticipating.

I nodded. "There've been others. Last one, Leo picked, which made him primary and me secondary.

He fell for her, and then she disappeared one day, breaking his heart. He still hasn't gotten over it."

She sighed. "I'm surprised he wants to do it again."

I shrugged. Who knew what went through Leo's brain. Yeah, he was my identical twin, but to be honest, in every other way we were polar opposites.

But I suspected he was thinking that getting back in The Game could be good for him. Especially being the secondary. Less responsibility.

"I don't know," she muttered as the last five of our thirty dishes were delivered.

I had to hand it to her, she was fucking gutsy about trying new food. Was she going to be gutsy about trying a new lifestyle?

"What don't you know, Echo?"

She shifted in her seat and looked around the restaurant boldly. I couldn't be sure, but something passed over her face.

Was it confidence?

Or determination?

"I don't know if I can eat any more tonight. Can we go home? And start The Game?"

CHAPTER 29

ECHO

Dᴜʀɪɴɢ ᴛʜᴇ ꜰʟɪɢʜᴛ ʜᴏᴍᴇ, my palms were sweating. In fact, I kept them plastered to the helicopter window and my seat so that Luca wouldn't try to hold my hand and realize what a mess I was.

Not ten hours earlier, I'd been on the lam, heading to the bus station with my packed up shit. I was getting the hell out of Las Vegas, probably never to return. I hadn't even been sure where I'd go. I was just getting on the first long-distance bus *somewhere*.

I hadn't known what The Game was, and I didn't care. I wasn't going to be controlled by a couple of mob bosses who wanted to restrict my coming and going. Who cared if they'd *saved* me? They could kiss my ass.

And now here I was, stuffed to the gills with expensive sushi, flying in a helicopter, and wearing a diamond necklace from Tiffany.

Holy crap.

And I was going to be *set for life.* I had no specifics on what that entailed, but if it meant my sister were going to be cared for, I was on board.

And it sounded like fun, too.

I didn't know what lay ahead that night, but I was curious as hell. And a little terrified.

What if it didn't go well? What if I sucked? What if I felt like a nasty slut?

What if it was awesome and I never wanted to see the light of day?

Smitt picked us up at the airport, and being his jovial self asked if we'd brought him any sashimi. I didn't have the heart to tell him I wasn't even sure what that was, although I'd probably just eaten it, with the multitude of courses Urasawa had served us.

God knew what all those dishes were. I didn't even ask. They tasted great, so why ruin it by finding out I was eating something like fish brains. Or testicles. I just didn't need to know that shit.

The helicopter ride had been mesmerizing in different ways. On the way to LA, it was still daylight, and the desert and mountains were incredible. No houses, no people. Just miles and miles of lonely landscape.

On the way home, it was dark save for a small sliver of moon, and because there was pretty much nothing on the ground below us, we were surrounded by pitch-dark. It was freaky to see no lights except for those on the actual helicopter.

But I felt safe with Luca, even if I were avoiding holding his hand.

After Smitt deposited us at the house, Luca led me straight to my bedroom. I wasn't sure what to expect, but I was feeling pretty sexy in my new duds, and with the way Luca had looked at me all night, I figured I'd managed to pull it together like a champ.

And my necklace! Cripes, if I didn't keep my hands off it, I'd wear it out. But it was beautiful and heavy and it had fucking *diamonds.*

Someone had given me diamonds.

I pushed my bedroom door open with Luca right behind me and found there were candles lit, small votive ones in glasses, on every surface of the room. Their light flickered up the walls and onto the ceiling like big, yellow tongues.

"You like it?" a voice said from the corner.

I shrieked. I couldn't help it.

Luca started laughing. "Relax, will you? It's my brother."

Well, shit. I didn't know part of this deal included people hiding in corners.

"Leo. Hello." I could barely make him out, sitting in the dark. Guess he got credit for the candles.

And in the dim light, I could see rose petals had been scattered over my bed.

Well. Chalk one up for Leo.

"Undress," he said, still from the corner.

What?

I put my hands on my hips. "*You* undress."

Now that my eyes had adjusted to the light, I saw the two guys exchange looks.

Oh Christ. Was this another rule thing that I was the last to know?

He got up and slowly walked toward me. Luca positioned himself behind me.

Oh lord. I wasn't down with another spanking.

Leo leaned close to me, so close I could feel his breath on my face. "I. Said. Undress."

I bent to take off my shoes, then lifted my halter over my head.

"Mmmm. Those tits," Leo said. "Keep going."

I unzipped my pants and slowly pushed them down, leaving my nude thong in place. I was as excited as I was nervous. What were they going to do with me? How was this supposed to work?

Why hadn't I watched more porn, like Yasmina had recommended all the time?

"That's what I'm talking about," Leo murmured, looking me up and down.

From behind, Luca's hands gathered my hair into one large hank. "She's gorgeous, isn't she, bro?" he growled.

I squirmed and shuddered under Luca's lips, brushing my skin from one shoulder to the next, leaving me vacillating between discomfort and euphoria.

Holy shit, I was with *two guys*.

With Luca kissing my back, Leo touched his lips to mine. We barely made contact, our breath warming each other's faces. Then, in a sudden movement, his mouth crashed into mine.

I'd never had a conversation with Leo, much less kissed him, even though I found him insanely sexy in a dark and brooding way his brother was not. So, to be taken by him so roughly, almost as if he were entitled to me, was so out of the norm aggressive and nasty that… I had to admit, I loved it.

He placed his hands on the sides of my face, cupping my cheeks, which was in gentle contrast to his bruising lips. From behind, Lucas reached around to knead my breasts, softly at first, then pulling on my nipples until I was in agony. That, mixed with Leo's rough kiss, made my legs tremble until I had to hold his shoulders to remain upright.

At least for the moment. I figured at some point we would no longer be standing.

Just a hunch.

Leo pulled back from my lips and looked at his brother over my shoulder. "What should we do with this lovely young lady, Luc?"

If they didn't do something soon, I was going to pass the hell out.

Luca steered me toward the edge of the bed and sat

me on its edge. I don't know why, but I snapped my knees together and folded my hands in my lap. I might have been nearly naked, surrounded by flickering candles, with two of god's most beautiful men gazing at me, but I sat as proper as a lady in church.

Who the fuck knew why.

The guys stepped back, looking me over like I was a piece of meat they were considering devouring. They murmured between themselves as I sat there like a good girl, and I couldn't help but wonder what it was like for them to have been essentially forced into their family 'business' when they were so young. Had they ever had the chance to think about other things they might have liked to do with their lives?

Maybe their 'privileges' were not *all that*.

But my musings were cut short by Leo, who positioned himself right in front of me. "Take out my cock."

His gruffness caught me off guard, and I just looked at him. And it seemed that moment was too long for his impatient ass.

He looked over his shoulder at Luca, who had taken a seat and was watching us with a smile. He turned back to me. "Haven't you ever sucked cock before?"

I rolled my eyes. "I'm not a goddamn virgin, for heaven's sake."

In the dim light I could see his eyes widen, and the smirk on his face grow. With his thumb and forefinger, he took hold of my chin. A little too tightly.

I tried to jerk away, but he held me tighter. But the moment I reached for his belt, he let me go.

"Good girl," he crooned.

Fishing through a tangle of shirttails and boxer shorts, I reached his cock, which was rock hard and… oh shit…

I couldn't even close my fingers around it.

I pulled him out and ran the soft skin of his head against my cheek. The sticky drop of precum smeared over my face, and when I finally got his cock in my mouth, the salty tang of it was delicious. I wanted more.

With a deep breath, I took as much of him in my mouth as I could, my hand lightly pistoning him at the root. When I glanced up at him with my watering eyes, he smiled and took hold of my head.

"How you doin' over there, bro?" Luca asked.

Leo groaned as I intensified the suction on his cock. "Fucking great. You want in on this?"

With my mouth full, I saw Luca making his way toward me, dropping his jacket and shirt on the floor, and opening his pants. By the time he reached me, he was butt naked, lightly fisting his cock, his gaze glued to mine.

Leo released my head and slowly withdrew from my mouth. As his brother got closer, he stepped aside.

I opened wide to take Luca, but he stopped and glanced at Leo. "What should we do with her now?"

Leo looked at me with dark eyes. "Lick her pussy."

My mouth snapped shut.

Luca smiled. He laid me back on the bed, propping my feet on his shoulders. As he bent, his fingers dove inside my wet pussy, and with his thumb on my clit, he began to make small circles.

I shimmied my hips in rhythm to his thrusting, and just when I was starting to moan, his lips moved to my clit. His tongue circled my nub, sending goose bumps rocketing over my body. Then he really zeroed in. I thought I was going to lose my mind.

"Oh my god, Luca, yes…" I murmured.

The bed moved and I opened my eyes to see Leo preparing to put his cock back in my mouth. I turned my head to take him, and he pushed to the back of my throat, initially causing me to choke and sputter. But I was finally able to move my head to piston him.

"Mmmm, suck me baby," Leo murmured. "And lick that pussy, Luca. I wanna see her come."

Luca pulled out from between my legs and looked up at me. "Does baby want to come?"

I could only groan with my full mouth.

He returned to my pussy, first licking me from clit to ass, where he worked a finger into my bum. I squirmed to take him deeper, and when he was finger-fucking my behind, he closed his lips on my clit again.

That was it.

I began to buck like a wild woman. I had to grip Leo's thighs so I didn't go flying off the bed. As I did, my mouth filled with his cum, some of it leaking back out onto my face and the bed beneath us.

"Fucking A," he shouted, pulling out of my mouth and spurting the rest on my tits.

He fell back on the bed, grabbing my hand and pulling it to his lips.

Just as I was coming down from my orgasm, Luca flipped me onto my stomach and straddled my hips. I heard a condom snap over his length, and he dipped himself between my legs until he reached my pussy. Constrained as I was, I pushed my ass back against him, and he slipped inside me to the hilt, stretching me to capacity.

"Hold her head, man," Luca said.

Leo pressed my face into the bed, turned just enough so I could breathe, and as my second orgasm rolled in, I pounded my hands against the bed.

"Oh god Luca, yes, fuck me please…" I wailed.

"So tight…" he groaned.

He got even harder inside me, if that were possible, and with one more unrelenting thrust, held himself deep. The throbbing of his orgasm set off another in me, hitting me with wave after wave, leaving me screaming until I was hoarse.

Holy shit.

I turned to my back, collapsing, Luca on one side of me and Leo on the other, holding hands with each.

"Wow," was all I could manage.

If that was The Game, I wasn't sure I'd ever want it to end.

"Fucking hot," Leo said.

"Seriously." Luca turned over to see me. "You're amazing, baby."

I smiled and squeezed my eyes shut, not wanting the moment to end. I'd just been ravished by two of the most beautiful men on the face of the earth.

Didn't get much better than that.

CHAPTER 30

ECHO

THE GUYS MUST HAVE SERIOUSLY WORN me out, because I woke hours later, although it was still dark, tucked under my fluffy down comforter. The candles had all been blown out, and Luca was just getting out of the bed.

Leo was gone. Guess sleeping with me was not part of The Game.

Luca kissed my temple. "I need to go take care of something," he whispered.

In the middle of the night?

"What?"

"Sal called me. I need to go."

"Well, okay. Be careful."

Being woken by your boss at god knows what hour in the middle of the night was not something I'd be too happy about, but I guess when you do the kind of work Luca did, you were always on the clock.

But to be honest, I didn't mind some time to myself after my threesome. I was quite happy to curl up in my own bed and snooze 'til the sun came up.

Only, I didn't sleep that long. Luca and Leo passed through my dreams, and the funny thing was, I couldn't tell them apart. Not at all. Luca's usual facial hair was gone, making it impossible to tell the difference between the two.

As I looked around, both brothers melded into one in my dream, and I couldn't tell who I was left with. I looked closer and closer, trying to figure it out until my eyes flew open and I stared into my dark bedroom.

My dark, and empty bedroom.

"Good morning, Mary," I said when I entered the kitchen.

She handed me a cup of tea. Peace offering?

Nah.

Hands on hips, she stood right in front of me. I'd never been so close to her before and hadn't realized how short she was. "Why didn't you and Mr. Borroni eat last night's dinner?"

"We went out."

"You know how long it took me to make that roast?"

Didn't know, didn't care.

But I would be nice. "Maybe you should bring this up with Luca, Mary. I didn't make the plans, either way. Not sure what to tell you. Maybe we can eat it tonight?"

I put an egg on to boil and poured myself some cereal to the chagrin of Mary. I knew she wasn't used to people making themselves at home in her kitchen, but truth be told, it wasn't *her* kitchen. It belonged to Luca and Leo.

So she could *suck it*.

My cell phone vibrated in the pocket of my bathrobe. It was Dini.

"Hey, little sis. How are you?" I asked, stepping to the corner of the kitchen for a modicum of privacy.

What would Dini think of the guys' sprawling house? And what would she think of what had happened last night?

Actually I would never share that with her. She was way too innocent to know about some of the shit I did.

"Hi, Echo. I wanted to tell you that Tommy is getting married."

Ugh. My stomach dropped at the mention of my high school sweetheart. Another reason I thanked god that I'd exited that shit town.

I cleared my throat. Why I gave a crap about that dirtbag, I had no idea. "Really? To who?"

"The minister's daughter, Holly. Remember her?" she asked.

Seriously?

"Yeah. Yeah, I do. Well, good for them. Although how'd he snag her? I'd think he was the last guy on earth a minister's daughter would go for."

"Same way a guy like that would get any girl to walk down the aisle with him. She's pregnant," Dini said.

My egg timer went off, but I couldn't move. Mary rolled her eyes and turned off the stove.

"I hope they're very happy. Hey, I wanted to continue our conversation of yesterday, so I'm glad you called."

"Oh. Right," she said flatly.

Shit.

"Are you waffling on coming out here, Dini? I need you to be honest with me."

She was silent for a moment.

"I'm just not sure about leaving Mom," she said quietly. "She told me she doesn't know what she'd do without me."

For heaven's sake, the woman disappears for days, leaving Dini with nothing to eat. If it weren't for me, the poor thing would be malnourished, or worse. Apparently it wasn't enough that my mother had ruined her own life. Now she had to ruin Dini's.

I needed to talk to Luca. He'd offered to help with my situation, and it was time to call in that favor.

CHAPTER 31

LUCA

It was a power play.

A big, goddamn power play.

Sal had called me in the middle of the night and told me he had to see me. It wasn't the first time we'd had business to take care of at fucking zero dark thirty —that's how things rolled in Vegas, especially in our line of business—but I was not happy about leaving Echo's warm bed.

Jesus, the session Leo and I had with her was hot. She did great, as I knew she would, giving as good as she got. I could tell Leo was mesmerized, too, and that he wouldn't have minded being primary with her. But that was tough shit. She was mine.

I'd found her, and I got the coveted primary slot. He

was secondary, and that would change over my dead body.

That's how The Game was played.

I'd been secondary with the last woman, which worked out fine for me. Unfortunately for Leo, he fell in love, and his possessiveness drove her away. As Smitt always said, keeping them in a cage is a kink that works for only so long.

I felt for Leo, I really did. He'd never allowed himself to get close to a woman before, and when he finally did, she tore his heart out and shit on it. It wasn't pretty. He was so on edge during that time, he nearly beat one of our enemies to death with his bare hands. I was the only one who could stop him, and afterward, he didn't remember a thing.

I doubted he'd ever fall for anyone again. That's how defended the poor bastard was.

But that didn't mean he didn't fuck around like a rabbit.

Among all our other businesses, we owned a very special, very private, and very expensive club, where very adult things happened.

Yup, a sex club.

Vegas had plenty of those to choose from, mostly catering to weekend tourists who wanted to take a walk on the wild side and do some things they'd *never* do at home.

Our club wasn't really for those folks.

Our club was for the committed. And I hoped I might introduce Echo to it at some point.

Leo got his rocks off there on a regular basis. He'd been busting my balls that I hadn't been since we'd taken in Echo, but I was far more interested in her than any of the regulars at the club. The women there were stunning and sexy as hell, but not one of them had ever caught my interest the way Echo had.

And that was fine with me, even if it annoyed the shit out of my brother.

The Game was an outgrowth of our club activities. Before we brought it home, we'd choose a woman a couple of times a year and flip to see who was primary and who was secondary. Just as the rules still dictated, whoever got primary got to fuck the lucky lady first by himself, and then the secondary could have dibs but only as a threesome. When word got out in the club that we were playing this way, everyone else began to copy us, and that took some of the fun out. It wasn't until Leo thought to invite someone home and stay with us awhile that we *really* got into it.

And now we were playing with Echo, who was fucking amazing. Getting out of her bed in the middle of the night had pissed me the hell off.

Sal had me meet him at the office. There was one good thing about driving across Vegas in the wee hours of the morning—no traffic.

I settled into a chair opposite Sal's desk, careful not to get too comfortable. I didn't want to start nodding off in his face if he was going to drone on about something I found only marginally interesting.

"What's up, Sal? Are the Russians at it again?" I asked.

The Russian syndicates had been a thorn in our sides since they'd arrived on the scene. Most new 'business' in Vegas knew to stay in their lane. Our territories were clearly demarcated. But the Russians like to push the boundaries, both literal and figurative, which meant that we had to occasionally smack them down.

Sal leaned forward, elbows on his desk, and took a long draw on the special tea he had shipped over from China. He must go through pounds of the shit every year. I didn't know how he did it—the goddamn stuff stunk to high heaven.

"I wanted to talk to you about the girl."

No. Fucking. Way.

He woke me up in the middle of the night to bust my balls about *Echo*?

Fine. He could play that way if he wanted. I was irritated but wasn't about to let him know.

"Tell me about your concerns," I suggested. This way I could buy time to think about the most constructive way to deal with his manipulative bullshit.

I didn't like going against Sal's wishes. I owed the guy. Both Leo and I did. But I wasn't accommodating a ridiculous request.

He'd just have to get over it.

He shared his usual reservation that having her

around would be a distraction, but as he spoke further, he reiterated how he believed her to be a security risk. As the only living witness to the hit at Loaded Dice, he wanted her out of the way.

I knew what *out of the way* meant, and he knew better than to go there. He figured he was being generous by offering to give her some cash and make her leave town. But if it had been anyone else, that would have been the end of their life. Over and out. It was fortunate Leo had gotten rid of the other women there, the strippers, before anything went down. They'd be facing the same fate.

CHAPTER 32

LUCA

WHEN I GOT BACK HOME, it was too late to go back to bed, but too early to do anything else, so I went down to the gym for my daily hour-and-a-half workout. I was just getting into my zone on the treadmill when Echo came down the stairs bundled in her robe and fluffy slippers.

Without a trace of makeup and her hair in knots from the previous night's play, she was sexier than I'd ever seen her. My workout was in danger of being cut short very quickly.

"Morning, beautiful. How are you feeling?"

A slight blush washed over her face as she looked around the gym, avoiding my eyes.

But then she got her chill back.

"Whew. What an amazing night." Her gaze was

steady on me, and I wondered if she'd come down hoping for more of what she'd just had the night before.

And this time, I'd have her to myself.

"Hey, I was thinking. It's kind of boring to just hang around the house all day, and when I leave on my own, that seems to be causing problems. So, what can I do?"

I thought for a sec. "I'll schedule you a spa day. How's that sound?"

Her eyes widened. "I've never had a spa day. Sounds awesome."

"I'll set it up and have Smitt take you."

She clapped her hands and jumped up and down. "Oh my god, thank you. I'm gonna run upstairs and get ready."

"Okay," I called after her. "They don't open for a few hours, so just chill for now."

I slowed the treadmill so I could send a text to the manager at the spa in our best hotel. I was going to make sure this day was special. I needed to keep Echo occupied since she wasn't a sit-around-on-her-ass kind of woman. 'Course, this was only one day, and something more long-term was called for. But this was a start.

I could always give her a job at one of my boutiques. She liked pretty clothes. Give her something to do in a place where I could easily keep an eye on her and keep her safe.

The spa manager had followed my instructions to a T. My girl had been given the red-carpet treatment with a facial, waxing, mani-pedi, and some other body treatments she asked for which I'd never even heard of.

Women liked that shit.

So when it was time for the grand finale—the massage—the manager sent me a quick text as a heads-up, and I drove the half mile to the hotel.

"Mr. Borroni, good to see you," the manager said, leading me to the men's locker room and handing me a pile of folded garments. "Here are some clothes for you to change into. Please let me know if we can get you anything else."

I was going to have to speak to the hotel management about giving that woman a raise.

I slipped into the white cotton drawstring pants and tunic I'd been given and headed over to the spa's most luxurious massage room, which the manager had brilliantly made sure to set aside for Echo.

I opened the door to a dimly lit room playing quiet relaxation music. A male masseuse was kneading Echo's back as she lay with her face in the head cradle. As I got closer, I could hear her steady breathing. She was enjoying it.

And I was about to make her feel even better.

I tapped the masseuse, who'd been briefed on my plan. He nodded silently and left the room.

I oiled up my hands and began making long strokes on Echo's back, unbeknownst to her. I wasn't a masseuse by any stretch of the imagination but I'd had enough massages to fake it for a few minutes.

I leaned into the muscles of Echo's back and gradually eased the sheet covering her ass down to her thighs. Then I bent close to her ear.

"Hey, gorgeous."

Her head popped up, and as she realized it was me, a huge smile spread across her face.

"Hey! You're cheating me out of my massage, you brat," she laughed.

"Is that what you think? We'll see about that."

She sighed and returned her face to the cradle as I poured more of the lightly scented oil into my hands. I ran them up and over her curvy ass cheeks and squeezed them, getting closer to the area between her legs. She moaned lightly and spread her legs a couple of inches.

Squeezed between her luscious thighs was her beautiful, shaved pussy, and she gasped when I ran my oiled fingers up and down her slit. I parted her puffy lips to see her more fully, and I swear, my cock was so fucking hard I could barely stand.

I worked my oiled fingers inside her, and she spread her legs further, pushing back against me for more. Her breathing got raspy, and I knew she was getting close.

"Oh, Luca," she said, grinding against my hand.

"You good, baby?" I asked.

"I want it in my ass, Luca. Please."

Well, damn. She didn't need to ask twice.

I slipped my oily finger out of her pussy and pressed it against her pretty asshole. I'd totally gotten off on watching her tighten against my plundering fingers the night before, and I was fucking psyched she was asking for more.

As I slipped a finger into her ass, I made small circles on her clit with my other hand to help her relax. Once I had two fingers in her, and she was pushing against my hand for more, I dropped my drawstring pants and crawled up on the table. With a fistful of oil, I greased up my dick and positioned it against her ass.

"You ready?" I asked.

She pushed her bum up in the air like a little beggar. "Please. Now."

"Okay. Push out a bit." I pressed my cock against her, and when she pushed, I was able to ease my head in.

She gasped.

"You okay?"

She was breathing heavily. "I think so. I'm ready for more."

"Push against me, baby," I said so she could drive.

As she moved, I slid in almost all the way. She was taking my cock like a champ. I'd never dreamed my little cocktail waitress would love ass sex.

She clenched me so hard it almost hurt. I squirted more oil where I was sliding in and out and then leaned forward so my lips were next to her ear.

"Squeeze me baby. Squeeze me with your ass."

"Uh… uh… I'm coming," she whispered as she trembled beneath me.

Her orgasm set off my own, and with one more deep pump, I filled her ass.

As soon as we'd caught our breath, I got a warm towel and wiped her down. I helped her to her feet and guided her over to the room's Japanese soaking tub. I followed her into it, and we were silent for a few minutes. When she leaned against me in the tub and nestled her head into me, I knew it was time to talk.

"Echo, why is your sister in a wheelchair?" I asked.

"I'd been wanting to talk to you about that," she said.

She took a deep breath and told me one of the most incredible stories I'd ever heard, from the loss of her dad, to her sister's diagnosis, to her grandmother's death.

I mean, everyone has a story. I knew I sure as hell did, with the disappearance of my dad and murder of my mom. But I had people and resources to fall back on.

Echo had none of that and had thus ended up in Vegas, a town where people bring their dreams, and if they are lucky, they don't leave completely broken.

"Your mom sounds pretty out of it."

She nodded. "Mmmm. That's on a good day. And it drives me crazy that one, Dini is subject to that, and two, that she's so damn loyal to a horrible mother who'd let her starve to death before she'd lift a finger for her."

"We gotta get her out of that situation. I mean, Vegas isn't the best place for an innocent like your sister, but she'd be miles better off than she is right now," I said.

"Yeah. So now you know why I'm kind of obsessed."

I pulled my arms around her and kissed her wet hair. "I'd be the same way about my sibling."

"Yeah, my ultimate dream is to get her out here so we can open a little breakfast diner, just like the one we used to go to with Gran when we were kids."

Her eyes widened in a way I'd never seen.

She continued breathlessly. "Tourists and locals alike would come, and everyone would love it. We'd be famous for pie. All kinds of pie."

I'd be lying if I didn't say I was moved by the pureness of her aspirations.

I pushed the wet hair off her forehead. "I know you want something to do with your days. I was thinking of seeing if you wanted to work in one of my boutiques. But now that I hear you talking, I wouldn't mind investing in a 'straight' business—one with no ties to my other world. And there's a part of town that's just now being developed that might welcome the addition of an old-school diner."

She turned to look at me. "Really? You think it's a good idea?"

"Potentially. We could crunch some numbers."

She laughed. "Well, I don't know how to 'crunch numbers,' but I'd like to learn."

"Yeah?" I asked, turning her to face me and wrapping her legs around my waist in the water. "How's your bottom feel?" I asked, sprinkling kisses over her temples.

She shimmied on my lap. "Um. A teeny bit sore. But I think I'll be okay."

I kissed her lips. Her sweet, sweet lips.

Yeah. If Sal thought I was giving this one up, he was fucking crazy.

I'd finally won the jackpot I'd been trying for all my life.

CHAPTER 33

ECHO

As time passed, I realized spending my days reading, working out, and lying by the pool wasn't all that bad. I wouldn't want to do it forever, so I looked at it as a sort of vacation. One where I got paid, according to the rules of The Game.

What a lady of leisure I'd become, too. It had taken a little getting used to—I was never one to sit around on my ass, but I told myself it was only for three months, and then I'd have the freedom—and money— to do whatever the hell I wanted. Smitt had shown me how to work out with weights, and Mary and I were just staying out of each other's way.

And I could always get a job at one of Luca's boutiques if I got bored.

Luca had never specified what 'set for life' meant,

and I'd never asked for details. I guess I just trusted him. Regardless, I had plenty of time to think about what I was going to do once I'd been sprung from my gilded cage.

First, I'd find a nicer place to live than what Yasmina and I currently had. Which would not be too hard, considering the present place was pretty much a shithole. Maybe we'd find an apartment in a complex with a pool and some nice palm trees for shade. Or maybe even rent a house so we'd have our own pool.

Then, I'd fly back to West Virginia and get my sister. I didn't care if I had to drag her kicking and screaming, I'd get her on a plane, wheelchair and all, and bring her to Vegas.

First order of business would be to get her to the best doctors in town, which again wasn't saying much considering the nasty little place we came from. I'd have them evaluate her and make sure she was getting the best physical therapy money could buy.

I could even send her to college. She'd always been the smart one in the family, easily earning straight A's and reading everything she could get her hands on.

I guess you could say I was a bit obsessed with making up to Dini all the shit she'd had to deal with by being stuck with my mom.

Like I'd always said, some people got the shitty end of the stick, and some people got the even shittier end —that would be my little Dini.

If there was enough money—who the hell knew

what the guys would throw my way—I'd look into kicking off that diner I'd always dreamed about. That was probably a pretty big long shot, though—restaurants required a lot of money to get going, and while I thought Luca would be generous as evidenced by all the clothes and things he'd given me, I highly doubted he planned to finance a restaurant on my behalf.

But that was okay. The money would buy me some time to figure out what I wanted to do with my life once I got Dini set up. For now, I planned to enjoy living in a massive modern home with two of the most beautiful men the universe had ever created, with all the pretty clothes and leisure time I never imagined I'd have.

I was sitting out by the pool with my copy of the latest *People* magazine when the doorbell rang. Then, when it rang again, I realized no one else was going to answer it, so I got off my ass.

I padded through the house in my bikini, only dripping slightly on the polished concrete floors, and opened the door to a delivery person with a giant silver garment bag. Of course, it was for me.

"Sign here," the courier said, shoving a clipboard in my face.

When he was gone, I ran up the stairs to my room and tore at the bag like a little animal. I didn't know what had gotten over me, but the gifts that Luca chose for me had become the highlight of my days. It was as if, for a brief moment, someone cared enough about me to consider what I might like. He wanted to make me happy and was even courting me in his own way.

His gifts were always accompanied by a note that said something like 'wear this tonight,' or 'see you at such-and-such-a-time.'

And the were breathtaking, like the one I was currently opening.

The silver garment bag contained a stunning evening gown fitted around the bust, which flared out with several handkerchief layers of chiffon underneath —barely enough to keep the dress from being see-through.

Included were matching Louboutin sling-back pumps, a red Chanel lipstick, and, of course, a note.

I knew this would be incredible with your black hair
Wear the lipstick
See you at 7

All the assumptions made by the note—that I'd be available and ready and waiting—were so erotically charged that I was dizzy for a moment. There was a light tingling between my legs, and I shifted happily inside my bikini bottom.

My gig as a mafia princess was going to be short-lived, but it was turning out to be fun while it lasted.

CHAPTER 34

ECHO

By the time seven rolled around, I'd been ready to go for an hour. I'd blown my hair out in long waves and wore a sexy-as-hell smoky eye. My lips were red as cherry, and the almost-sheer dress barely concealed the dark outline of my nipples and the shadow of my shaved pussy.

At a glance, someone might think *oh, I almost see her privates*. But if they looked hard and long enough, they'd realize they actually *could* see my privates. I couldn't wait for Luca's reaction.

I was pacing off my excited energy and wandered through the kitchen.

Mary put her hands on her hips. "You want something to eat before you go out?"

Holy shit. While not effusive, it was by far the nicest thing she'd ever said to me.

"Oh. Thank you. Maybe something super light."

She pulled open the fridge and dug around. "You want a little broth? That would tide you over but keep you looking good in that dress." She looked me up and down and nodded in approval.

Wow. Guess she and I had reached some sort of peace agreement.

"Oh my god, that sounds perfect, thank you," I said.

I was sipping my warm broth from a mug, not wanting to sit down if I could avoid it, when Smitt showed up.

"Echo, you ready?"

I put my mug in the sink to stay on Mary's good side. "Yeah. Is Luca here?"

He shook his head. "He wants me to bring you to the gallery. He was stuck at work late."

Oh. I'd never been to a gallery. Not a real one anyway. Just the pawnshops that acted like they were galleries but were mostly just full of crap.

"We're going to a gallery?" I asked.

"Yup. It's one of the businesses the guys own."

I followed him to the car, where he opened the back door for me. "I can sit up front with you, I don't mind."

He shrugged. "Let's be fancy. You take the back seat."

I laughed. "Okay, boss." I climbed in, careful to

smooth out the chiffon layers to keep my outfit as perfect as possible.

As we drove across town, I couldn't help but wonder why Luca wanted me to meet him, rather than come to pick me up himself. When we pulled up in front, there was a carpet that reached from the curb to the building's front door, just like in the awards shows I'd watched on TV. And what was even crazier was that on one side, there were a bunch of people taking pictures of the guests.

I really didn't want my picture taken.

Smitt extended his hand for me to exit the car. "Hold your head up and smile. That's all you have to do. Luca is waiting for you."

I grabbed his hand in both of mine. "Thank you, Smitt."

He winked at me and sent me on my way.

Smile, don't trip, smile, don't trip, I chanted to myself as I ran the gauntlet in front of flashing light bulbs and people hollering things like, "Who are you?" and "What is your name?"

The brief walk from the car to the gallery felt like it took forever, but when I neared it, the door flew open, and Luca was standing right there, wearing a deliciously sexy grin.

He eyed me up and down.

"Holy fuck. Look at you," he growled quietly.

He took my hand before the doors closed

completely, but not fast enough to miss the questions being thrown our way.

"Luca, who's the mystery woman?"

"Got a new girl, Mr. Borroni?"

"Employee or date?"

He smiled and waved briefly at the question throwers before the doors closed and drowned them out.

He leaned close to my ear. "I'm trying not to stare."

I elbowed him. "Cut it out. You're silly." Despite my efforts to act cool, I felt a warm blush wash over my face, and turned away as best I could to hide it.

He led me to the bar, and while I was waiting for my flute of champagne, he ran his hand over my ass. "No panties. I knew I didn't need to ask you."

I smacked his hand away just to be sassy. But truth be told, I liked him feeling me up. He *wanted* me, and I liked that.

"Thank you for this amazing dress," I said, raising my glass to him. "I feel like a princess."

Our gazes locked with an intensity that was hard to put into words. In any other circumstance with anybody else, it would have been painfully awkward. But with Luca, it was… like magic.

"Would you two losers stop making eyes at each other?"

I turned to find Leo. "Hey. How are you?"

He responded by rolling his eyes with his usual smirk and wandered away, scotch in hand.

My arm hooked through Luca's, he and I did a couple laps around the gallery, and damn if I didn't feel like a million bucks. Heads were turning everywhere we walked, and Luca was the perfect gentleman about introducing me to the people he knew. I got a lot of stares from other women, but I supposed that was to be expected. He and his brother were not only deadly handsome, but it hadn't been hard to figure out they were also pretty damn powerful. There were clearly some women at the party who would have liked to be in my place.

It was a beautiful, glittering crowd, with nearly every woman in sequins and man in a tux. Silent waiters floated among the crowd with platters of foods I couldn't begin to identify. Not that it mattered. No one was eating, anyway.

But they sure were drinking. The trays of champagne were emptied almost as fast as they were being brought from the kitchen.

"Hey, does anyone here know about The Game?" I asked Luca quietly.

"Nope. And let's keep it that way," he said, bending to kiss my temple and sending a wave of goosebumps across my skin.

The gallery was in a rustic old building that must have been industrial at one time. The floor was of warped wood planks, and the walls were exposed brick. A wide set of stairs led up to what I guess you would call a mezzanine, where people mingled and looked down over the first floor.

"Want to go up there? Check it out?" Luca asked.

I loved that he paid attention.

CHAPTER 35

ECHO

ONCE UPSTAIRS, I realized *that* was where most of the art was on display, and I stopped in front of one huge painting that caught my eye.

"Is that what Vegas was like back in the day?" I asked. It looked like an interpretation of photographs I'd seen when the town was just a few dusty streets and casinos, with giant neon signs and marquees announcing star-studded shows.

It was utterly charming in a vintage old-school way.

Luca leaned back on his heels, nodding.

"Hey, have you lived here in Vegas all your life?" I asked.

"Yeah. I always thought I'd leave, but I never got around to it."

I wanted to ask where he might have gone, had he

been free to leave. But something about his face said to drop it.

He took my hand. "I want to show you something."

We arrived in front of a white, nondescript door. Pulling a key out of his pocket, he unlocked it and pushed it open. I poked my head inside while he flicked on a low light. He followed me in, closing the door behind us.

"What do you think?" he asked, looking around.

He pointed at a window overlooking the gallery below where we could watch the party. It was quite the rush to see it from this perspective and yet be removed from the hustle and bustle and noise.

"It's like seeing a movie with the sound turned off," I said.

I craned my neck to see more of the party below as Luca walked up behind me. He lifted my dress, and running his hands up the back of my thighs, pushed aside the layers of chiffon to get his hands on my bare ass.

The heat that had been building between my legs turned into a full-on throb, and my breath caught as he ran his fingers over my pussy lips.

"Mmmm," was all I could manage.

"Looks nice too, with those high heels and bare ass," he murmured.

I spun around to face him and made quick work of his fly. I had to get my mouth on his cock, and knowing there was a raging party just feet away made it that much naughtier.

I crouched and ran my tongue up his long erection, licking the drops of precum from his head. I wrapped my lips around it and enjoyed my little bit of heaven.

"Whoa, baby. You're gonna make me come right here."

Pulling back, I looked up at him. "That's the whole idea. I want you to come, in my mouth, and then we'll get back to the party. No one will be any the wiser."

He smiled down at me. "That's what I like to hear."

He put his hands on either side of my head. I reached for his ass cheeks, and pulled him toward me. I relaxed my throat so I could take as much of him as possible, and in minutes he groaned, his muscles tensing under my grip. He shoved his hips toward me one more time.

"Fuck, baby, fuck, I'm coming," he growled.

I swallowed everything he had to give, being sure to lick him clean. Couldn't have him going back to the party all sticky and stuff.

"You dirty, dirty girl," he said, laughing, and looking very, very happy.

I raised an eyebrow at him. "You complaining?"

"Fuck no, baby."

Our fingers wove together, and on our way back to the main floor, I found that the painting I'd liked was gone. In its place was something similar, but much smaller and not nearly as interesting. Darn.

Like I was going to buy it, anyway.

"That didn't last long, did it?" I asked.

"The good ones always get snapped up."

Once downstairs, I excused myself for the ladies' room. And by some stroke of luck—or not—I ran into someone I knew.

"Echo!"

I whipped around to see one of my fellow waitresses from Loaded Dice.

Holy shit.

I never thought I'd run into someone from there.

My heart thumped in my chest. How much did she know?

"Oh my god, Lori! How have you been?" I asked.

She looked around nervously. "I'm good, but I've been lying low. One of my friends dragged me out of the house tonight to this thing. I've been afraid to go out during daylight hours." She chugged the last of the champagne she was holding.

"Why? What's wrong?"

"Don't you know? That hit at the club—thank god I wasn't working that day—was carried out by the worst crime family in Vegas. I'm still freaked about the whole thing. I mean, how do we know they won't come for the rest of us? Aren't you scared?" She was squeezing my arm so hard it was starting to hurt.

I hadn't been afraid, but since she put it like that, my stomach acid began to churn, and suddenly the couple of glasses of champagne I'd had didn't feel like they'd gone down too well.

I decided not to mention to her that the crime family she spoke of was hosting me. And fucking me.

I nodded and looked around, too. "Yeah, Lori. We gotta be careful. Hey, I'm running to the ladies' room. You take care, okay?"

"Yeah. You too."

I slammed the bathroom stall door and sat down with my head in my hands. Was I getting in over my head? Was I playing with fire?

Fuck.

When I'd touched up my lipstick, finger-combed my hair, and taken several deep breaths, I exited the restroom and walked right into Smitt.

"Oh hey. Sorry about that," I said. "Didn't know you were here."

He nodded. "I've been watching from a distance. You know, just to make sure everything's okay."

"Oh. Thank you."

He looked around and lowered his voice. "I heard you talking to that girl over there." He gestured with his thumb.

I looked back for Lori, but she was long gone. In fact, the crowd was beginning to thin.

"Lori? Yeah, I used to work with her at Loaded Dice. She's really nervous since everything went down."

'Yeah. I heard. What about you? Are you nervous?"

I took a deep breath as I thought about how to answer the question and nodded slowly. "To be honest, I wasn't. But when I saw the fear in her eyes, it was contagious. And I guess I am a little freaked-out now."

He steered me off to a corner where we could still see Luca talking to some people. "You are right to be scared. You'd be stupid not to be."

"Really?" My legs were suddenly wobbly. I wanted to go home. My real home. With Yasmina. And to crawl into my crummy little twin bed and stay there for a long time.

"Yes, Echo. But the thing is, you are safe with us. You are always safe with us. For the time being, just stay close to home, and for heaven's sake—follow the rules. They're designed to keep you safe. And that'll keep the brothers happy, too."

Well, shit. Message received.

They didn't have to worry about a thing.

I wasn't going anywhere.

CHAPTER 36

LUCA

I CRANED my neck to see through the crowd. What the hell was taking Echo so long to get back? But when I saw her chatting quietly with Smitt, I felt better knowing he was looking out for her.

Unfortunately, I was trapped by a couple of bitchy gossips whose husbands were part of my organization, and who were getting on my last nerve.

"So, Luca," the one with the big fake tits said, "who's the girl? Do you *like* her?"

The second one giggled, batting her eyelashes. "Or are you just *fucking* her?"

They looked at each other and broke into giggles, entirely unaware of what idiots they were, and entirely unaware of how they were irritating the shit out of me.

I rubbed my eyes. It was late and I couldn't help

myself. I was also out of patience with other human beings and was moments away from telling these women to go fuck themselves.

"Seriously, Luca," she said, rubbing on my arm, "she looks like she just fell off the turnip truck."

Really? Were they *really* going there?

Fuck them. They were about to learn a hard lesson.

"Tell me, ladies, have you enjoyed tonight's party?"

"Oh yes."

"Very nice."

They nodded enthusiastically.

"Good. I'm glad you enjoyed it, because this is the last one you'll be attending. As of tonight, both your husbands are no longer employed with Borroni & Sons. They will be told formally in the morning, but if you feel like sharing the news with them this evening, be my guest."

"Wha... Luca, what do you mean?"

"Your husbands are fired. Effective, now."

Their faces were worth the price of admission. While their mouths hung slack and they paled beneath their layers of makeup, I turned to find Smitt and Echo walking toward me.

"Ready to head out?" Smitt asked us.

I took Echo's hand and gestured toward the door. "Lead the way, my man."

CHAPTER 37

LUCA

"I KNOW WHAT TODAY IS," I said.

Echo looked up from the grapefruit she was having for breakfast and blushed lightly. "Huh? What do you mean?"

"Mary," Leo hollered from the breakfast table where we were gathered.

She entered the dining room carrying a pie lit with three birthday candles.

One for each of us.

"Happy birthday, baby," I said as Mary set the pie down and disappeared.

Echo was grinning ear to ear. "Are you guys kidding? You knew today was my birthday?" She shook her head, laughing.

"You might not realize it, Echo, but Luca and I know a lot of shit."

"Shall I make a wish?" she said, looking hungrily at the pie.

"You probably should, although I think I know what you're wishing for."

She wrinkled her nose at me and closed her eyes.

Of course I knew what she was wishing. Well, not specifically, but I was certain it had to do one way or the other with her little sister.

And I loved that about her.

Very few people I knew were able to keep their eye on the ball the way Echo was. Her singular commitment to seeing things through for her sister blew me away. How many siblings make taking care of another their life's work?

Christ, would my brother do that for me?

"You know how I love pie! It looks incredible. Let's have some. I don't care that it's breakfast." She picked up a knife and dished out three generous pieces, leaving a fourth in the pie dish. "I gotta save some for Smitt."

She dove in, moaning with every bite at the peach blueberry pie Mary had made.

"Damn I think we'd better hide our slices before Echo here hoovers them up," Leo said.

She rolled her eyes.

I reached under the table for two large shopping bags.

"What are those?" she asked, inhaling her last bite.

"Birthday gifts. Have at it."

She pulled everything out of the bags and sat there before her pile of wrapped gifts, like a kid at Christmas.

Her eyes grew wide and I could swear they were looking a little watery. "I've never had gifts like this," she said, shaking her head in amazement. "My gran never had the money."

She ran her fingers over the pretty wrapping paper and twirled the boxes' curly ribbons between her fingers, as if being given the gifts was more momentous than the actual gifts.

It hadn't been easy to shop for Echo. Not because she was a difficult woman, but rather because we were already in the habit of giving her expensive gifts for no reason at all.

"Oh my god," she said, opening a flat velvet box. She slipped a diamond bangle over her hand, and it hung beautifully on her wrist.

She stared at it for so long, I had to encourage her to keep going.

She plowed through several other boxes of trinkets and luxury items, and when she was done, I pulled the last gift from its hiding place under the table.

"Check this out. It's huge," she said, tearing at the paper.

"Holy shit!" she screamed. She looked between Leo

and me. "You got me the painting from the gallery. The one I loved."

She jumped to her feet and screamed again. "Oh my god, thank you!"

She gave me a kiss, then ran to Leo.

Only Leo pulled her into his lap and reached his hand inside her robe to grab her tit. Their mouths fell together, and her arms circled his neck.

Fucking hot.

I stuck my head in the kitchen and asked Mary to run out to the store to get more coffee.

"But Mr. Borroni, we have plenty of coffee."

I tipped my head at her and widened my gaze.

"Oh," she said. "Okay." She hung her apron in the pantry, grabbed her purse, and left by the side door.

By the time I came back, Leo already had Echo on her back on the dining table, her bathrobe completely open. His face was buried in her pussy, and she was writhing. I took my seat and watched the show.

Echo's face was so beautiful I could hardly tear my gaze from it. Leo was working her pussy from her clit to asshole and back while reaching to pinch and pull her nipples.

Just before she started to come, he took two fingers and began to pump her pussy.

And that was all she wrote.

"Oh god... oh god, Leo... " she moaned as an orgasm hit.

When she finished, Leo pulled her into his lap, a

move so tender it shocked me. But I didn't let on because I didn't want to make my brother feel self-conscious. I wondered if the nice and kind Leo I'd once known might be making his way back.

Echo reached her hand out for mine.

"Best birthday, ever."

"And it's still morning," I said.

"What does that mean?" she asked, looking between Leo and me.

I looked at my watch and stood. I hated to leave her, but I had to put in a full day of work.

But I'd be home in time for more fun.

"We wondered if you'd like us to take you to a special sort of club tonight."

She furrowed her brow. "What the hell is a 'special sort of club'?" she asked, using air quotes.

"People go there to have sex," Leo said.

Her eyes widened. "Oh. You told me about that place." She looked at me with a sly smile.

I shrugged. "We thought you might like it. No pressure."

She looked from one of us to the other. "Promise to hold my hand once we're there?"

CHAPTER 38

LUCA

OF COURSE, before evening rolled around, I had the staff at one of my boutiques bring me a couple racks of dresses to choose a special birthday outfit for Echo, which I then delivered to the house with a note to be ready at eight. I'd hoped to be home before then, but with the way work was going, getting out by then was going to be a challenge.

I needed to talk to Leo. We just had too many goddamn businesses to run. The problem was, extricating ourselves from any one of them was difficult if not impossible due to the way they were all intertwined. Which made the thought of opening a simple little diner with Echo, completely independent of our other enterprises, increasingly appealing.

Speaking of Echo, Sal hadn't made mention of her

in a while. I wasn't sure whether that was a good thing or bad, but I was on my guard. I'd never seen him as a threat before, nor felt any mistrust toward him, but hey, we weren't in the business we were in because we were softies. And because I'd been doing this shit since I was fourteen when my dad dragged me into it, I knew relationships could turn on a dime. And sometimes, those turns were fatal.

"Echo!" I hollered into the cavernous house when I got home.

I didn't want our girl showing up at the club alone. That wouldn't be cool, especially for a first-timer. Besides, it was her birthday, and I wasn't a dick that way.

Leo met me at the bottom of the stairs, where we waited, and when Echo made her way down, Leo muttered *holy shit* under his breath.

I'd chosen the perfect dress for her.

She descended the steps, her gaze alternating between the two of us. She sparkled in a short silver metallic dress that hugged her curves and showed off her toned legs. She'd piled her hair into some sort of messy confection at the base of her neck and was wearing the red lipstick I loved on her.

"Hey, guys. Take a picture. It lasts longer," she said, laughing.

She kissed Leo on the cheek and then me, her new diamond earrings brushing the top of her bare shoulders.

"I don't think a photo would do you justice," Leo said.

She took us each by the hand as we moved toward the door that Smitt held open. "Well, thank you for the dress. I just love it. Actually, thank you for everything. What a birthday this has been."

I kissed the back of her hand. "And to think we're just getting started."

I loved her appreciation, but it was we who should have been thanking her.

When we got to the club, we brought Echo to the lounge area to relax and get something to drink.

"This place is gorgeous," she said, admiring the exposed beams above and the lazy ceiling fans slowly spinning from them.

"What's upstairs?" she asked, looking from one of us to the other.

I shrugged. "Want to go see?"

Of course she did. That's why we brought her there.

I held her hand tightly as we made a lap around the floor. I could tell she was trying to play it cool, but her eyes were wide and her fingers had a death grip on mine.

It was to be expected. The first time at a sex club was overwhelming for most.

We paused as we walked by a sprawling round mattress with a woman on her knees and a man at either end of her, one in her pussy and one in her mouth. Filmy white curtains fluttered around them, blown by the movements of their threesome.

"Look familiar?" I whispered.

She nudged me and pressed her head against my shoulder. "So hot."

We walked the length of the room, passing over-stuffed sofas and mattresses of all shapes and sizes, some with people going at it like rabbits, and others with folks who were just getting warmed up. In one corner were two good-looking couples shyly flirting with each other, sizing each other up and deciding if they wanted to play together.

A statuesque waitress wearing only high heels and a thong panty approached us with a tray of champagne flutes. Echo eagerly grabbed one and watched the woman walk away, her ass cheeks jiggling just the tiniest amount as she walked.

"I see a good spot over there," Leo said, pointing.

He'd found an unoccupied sofa in a corner. When we got to it, still standing, he put his hands on either side of Echo's face, kissing her gently. She threw her arms around his neck, and pressed against him, the short hem of her dress rising even higher.

With Leo in front of her, I pressed up against her back and leaned toward her ear. "You doing okay, baby? Feeling good?"

"Yeah," she said, reaching back to pull me closer.

A couple of people on the other side of the room

had settled into chairs to watch us. I couldn't blame them.

It wasn't every day you saw identical twins devouring the most beautiful woman in the room. And to be honest, it was fucking hot to be watched with her.

Seemed like she might be getting off on it, too.

While the dress I'd chosen for her was no longer covering her ass, I slipped it the rest of the way over her lovely bum to get my hands on her heated flesh. I kneaded her cheeks and realized I was desperate to get my face in between them.

And yes, she'd neglected to wear panties.

I looked at Leo and gestured toward the sofa with my chin. Enough standing.

"Baby," I whispered in her ear, "get on your knees. Facing the sofa back."

She obeyed without a hint of self-consciousness, her lovely ass exposed for all to see. And as she knelt, she made sure to arch her back more fully to open herself for me.

Leo positioned himself behind the sofa and leaning over it, pulled his cock out, which she hungrily accepted.

Pushing her knees apart on the sofa, I ran my fingers through her slit, and as I suspected, she was soaked. She pushed into my hand when I made small circles on her clit, and I increased my speed while I pulled my cock out with the other. The view of her most private parts was a beautiful sight, her lips puffy with need and juices leaking and running down her thigh.

"You ready, baby? Ready for some cock?" I asked in her ear.

With her mouth full of Leo, all she could do was nod and wave her ass around. But that was all I needed.

I gradually slid my hard dick inside her, and she groaned from the fullness. With my hands on her ass cheeks, I spread her open so I could see my cock plundering her sweet pussy.

"I'm gonna fuck you hard now, okay?"

As she pushed her ass back against me, I pistoned her pussy until I felt her walls contract. At same time, Leo's head fell back and he thrust his hips into her face, moaning loudly. For purchase, she held on to his thighs, her nails deep in his flesh.

She opened her mouth to scream, Leo's cum spilling down her chin.

"Oh god, fuck me... I'm coming."

Her orgasm sparked mine, and I buried myself in her one last time, spurting hotly into her, my hands gripping her small waist for purchase.

When I pulled out, I realized we had a small audience, which scattered when we were done, I liked to think because they'd been inspired to get on with their own fucking.

I pulled Echo's dress down over her ass, and she flipped over to sit on the sofa, her head against its back and her eyes closed.

"Holy shit, this is the best birthday ever. You guys have worn me out."

"I think you've worn us out," Leo said, taking her hand and bringing it to his lips.

We caught our breath for a few minutes when Echo lifted her head.

"I'm exhausted. Can we go home now?"

CHAPTER 39

LUCA

Echo sat between Leo and me, holding each of our hands, as Smitt drove us home.

"How did you know I'd respond to you like I have?" she asked quietly.

Christ, she was so direct. It was refreshing.

I looked at her beautiful face. "I don't know, Echo. But I did."

It had been a fucking awesome night. One I'd never forget. And hopefully the first of many.

And just as Smitt steered us onto the freeway overpass, a black SUV with darkly tinted windows pulled up next to us.

A little too closely next to us.

"Smitt, you see that car on our right?" Leo asked calmly.

He nodded. "Yup. They've been on our tail for about two minutes."

"Smitt, give me your gun," Leo said.

"What's going on?" Echo asked, sitting up and looking around.

Just as Smitt handed Leo his firearm, the window of the SUV opened just enough for the muzzle of a gun to protrude.

"Smitt!" I yelled.

But he was already on it. He slammed on the brakes, leaving the SUV to continue speeding forward, the shot from its gun having fired into the air.

Leo opened his window and leaned out, targeting the car that was now in front of us. With one deafening shot, he shattered its back window. The SUV swerved and then veered sharply to the right, smashing through the guardrail, off the overpass, and to the road beneath us. A second later there was a loud crash.

It was barely louder than Echo's screaming.

Smitt picked up his speed.

"Fuck," I said. "Good work, you guys."

Echo had my hand in a death grip, all color having faded from her face. "Wha... wha... what just happened?"

"That's what's known as an attempted hit. Poor fools didn't know what they were up against."

She closed her eyes. "Was someone trying to kill us?"

"Unfortunately, yes, baby," I said.

"Who was it?" she asked.

Leo was already on his phone, alerting the rest of our team.

"My guess is the Russians. They're pissed at us for shutting down their card-counting operation."

"Yeah. I think it was just a matter of time 'til they tried something," Smitt added.

"I guess this is an example of the kinds of things you need to keep me safe from?" she asked, her eyes wide.

"Yup. Perfect example."

Hopefully it wouldn't happen again anytime soon. But Echo was surrounded by the best security team money could buy.

"Thanks for the quick reaction, guys," I said.

Smitt nodded from the front seat. "Only the best for Borroni & Sons."

CHAPTER 40

ECHO

How can one of the best nights of your life also be your worst?

I opened an eye and peeked out from under the down comforter to look around my room. I was alone, as I'd hoped I'd be, but I knew to take nothing for granted. With these people I was living with, who knew what the hell one could wake up to?

Fuck, and where was my bedside water? I never went to sleep without a glass on my nightstand. I pushed myself up slightly to stretch, and I was knocked flat on my back by a throbbing headache.

Jesus, had I had that much to drink?

No, I hadn't. I knew I hadn't.

I was still freaked out by *almost being killed*.

Some fucking birthday present.

I tried again to get up, this time with more care and patience, and I made it to the bathroom with my eyes barely open to dig up some extra-strength aspirin and cool water. Then I slithered back to bed, stepping over the remnants of the night before—a dress, some high heels, and matching earrings and a bracelet—and spotted my birthday gifts in a corner with my new painting propped against them. I still couldn't believe they'd gotten it for me.

When we'd arrived home the night before, I let the guys know I'd be sleeping alone. I needed time for myself, and to be honest I think they were relieved. Smitt, Luca, and Leo all seemed to want the time to process the evening's events just like I did.

So I escaped to my room, locked the door, undressed, and crawled into bed.

Someone had tried to kill us. The words repeated in my mind. They were making me sick.

It might have been just another day at the office for the Borroni brothers, but I was not cool with assassins.

At all.

Fumbling for my phone, I pulled it under the comforter and called Dini at home, where the sun would just be coming up.

"Echo! Happy belated birthday. You're up early. Or should I say late?" she said.

"Thank you. I got your message yesterday but didn't have time to call you back."

In the background, I could hear her wheeling around the house.

"Why are you up so early?" she asked. "Everything okay?"

"Oh yeah," I lied. "Just a little insomnia. How are things there?"

She sighed. "Same ole, same ole. You know how it is."

I couldn't believe what I was about to say.

"Dini, I'm thinking of coming back. Vegas is just a little too big for me."

She gasped. "Really? Are you serious? What happened? Something happened to you, didn't it?"

If she only knew. Which she never would.

A lump was building in my throat, and I forced myself to steady my voice. It wouldn't do for her to hear me upset.

"No, Dini. Nothing like that. I don't know, I guess I'm just thinking through my options."

"Echo, you can't come back. Please don't come back. You escaped. You got out of this crappy little town. If you come back, that will dash all my dreams of someday getting out."

"But last time we spoke, you were waffling on leaving. I thought you wanted to stay with Mom," I said.

"I don't know what I'm going to do. But I can't see you take a step back. You have to keep trying to make it work. Pursue your goals. Then, maybe someday I can follow you there."

Well, shit. There went my easy out.

When I said goodbye to Dini, I sank back into my bed. I considered texting Yasmina, but at four a.m., she'd definitely know something wasn't right.

I did like Luca and Leo. They were very decent to me, even if they were more or less extorting me with The Game.

And they were fucking sexy as hell.

I'd had threesomes!

I'd been to a sex club!

I'd even tried anal! And I liked it!

Good lord. What the hell was happening to me?

The question was, could I adjust to this lifestyle? I mean, what if they asked me to stay beyond the three months, which I was pretty sure Luca would. I could tell he liked me. A lot.

And I'd be lying if I said I didn't have feelings for him. I mean, he was one of the first people I'd ever met who hadn't pitied me when I shared my story. He accepted that life had dealt me some shitty hands and didn't get all dramatic or weepy over it. After all, he'd had his share of challenges.

He was generous, kind, and even kinky.

Guess that meant I was kinky, now, too.

And then the sex. I'd never known it could be like that.

I threw on some workout clothes and headed downstairs to the gym. Some time on the treadmill, and maybe even pounding on the punching bag, might help me throw off some of the stress caused by the night before.

But when I got there, Luca was doing weights, and through the large french doors, I saw Leo skimming the backyard pool.

"Hey. Why aren't you guys at work?"

"Because it's Saturday. Princess losing track of the days of the week?" He walked over and kissed my forehead.

Holy shit. I didn't even know what day it was anymore.

Christ, it seemed like just yesterday when I'd been worried about getting to work on time, where I served watered-down cocktails to men distracted by dancing naked women. I was living in a dumpy apartment, sleeping on a mattress that god only knew what had happened on in its long history, and had to limit my showers in order to leave a scrap of hot water for my roommate.

It wasn't that long ago.

"Why is Leo skimming the pool?" I asked, knowing they had someone to maintain it, just like everything else around the house.

Luca took the towel from around his neck and wiped down his face. "He likes it. Finds it mindless and soothing."

Huh. Learn something new about the guys every day.

"Why don't you go get a towel? We were going to take a swim."

I looked around the gym at the equipment that was calling my name and figured I could blow off my workout until later. A couple of laps in the heated pool would be nice.

But it seemed Luca and Leo had more than that in mind.

CHAPTER 41

ECHO

WEARING a bikini the guys had gotten me, and carrying my towel, I passed Mary in the kitchen. "Heading out for a swim," I said.

She looked up from her chopping. "Oh. I'll make myself scarce, then."

Huh?

"Why?"

"Luca and Leo don't usually wear bathing suits in the pool," she said with raised eyebrows.

I thought back to my first night in the house when I spied Luca skinny-dipping. I didn't know that was a regular thing.

Not that I had any objection.

The guys were already in the pool, so I dove into the deep end and started treading water.

"You must love having this at your disposal all the time," I said, swirling the water in front of me. I rolled to my back and looked up at the cloudless blue sky.

Could I get used to living like this?

Or had I already?

Luca swam up to me, and I wrapped my legs around his waist, leaning back in the water to float. His naked cock bounced against my leg, and I wriggled into it to torment him. Before I realized what was happening, he'd propelled us to the shallow end and propped me up on the edge of the pool.

"Open your bikini."

I pulled one of the ties on my hips, and the taut fabric fell away. I spread my legs to give the guys a good look.

"Take off the top, too," he said.

Untying the string behind my back, I pulled my top off with a glance toward the house. There was no sign that I was putting on a show for anyone but Luca and Leo, and I planned to keep it that way.

They moved close to me, staring hungrily at my pussy. It felt a little weird to be messing around outside, but what the hell—only the night before I'd been in a sex club and then almost been killed on the way home. Weird was my new normal.

"Let's see you lick her," Luca said.

Leo smiled up at me and buried his face between my legs, burrowing his tongue as deeply in my pussy as he could. I reached down to make small circles on my clit, and Luca growled.

"Fucking A, babe. Yeah, touch your pussy."

The warm morning sun and the two gorgeous men at my disposal were more than I needed. With Leo's tongue and my rubbing, I began to shudder.

"Oh… oh… fuck…" I moaned.

Leo's mouth moved off me. "Fuck her with your fingers, Luca," he said.

He entered me, pistoning my pussy until wave after wave of orgasm rolled over me.

"You are incredible, you know that?" Luca said.

Leo tapped my arm. "We had ulterior motives for inviting you for a swim this morning."

I rolled my eyes and laughed. "Really. Well, I'm shocked," I said mockingly.

He shrugged. "Hey, it's what you gotta do when you're secondary. It ain't easy. You have to resort to being a sly son of a bitch."

I leaned up on my elbow. "How'd you guys come up with The Game, anyway?"

"I don't know. It just evolved," Leo said, shrugging.

"It's rare we find someone we are both compatible with," Luca said.

I couldn't take my eyes off him. I had the strongest sense he wanted to say more but was holding back. Was it because Leo was there, or was it some sort of Game rule?

Leo dove under the water, and when he came up at

the other end of the pool, he called to me. "Echo, I think you're starting to like it here."

I flopped onto my back, the warm sun baking my naked body.

"I think you might be right. Assassination attempts notwithstanding."

CHAPTER 42

LUCA

THAT NIGHT, Leo and I did something we'd never done before.

We both piled into Echo's bed, intending to spend the entire night there with her.

I'd slept with Echo before, but Leo hadn't joined us. Theoretically, he could have, as long as I was there, but I figured he didn't like her enough to spend any extra time with her. He was still nursing his wounds from the last woman who'd played The Game. Maybe he always would be.

And maybe he was keeping some distance because he knew how smitten I was with Echo.

Some of Sal's men had investigated the shooting attempt on the freeway. Since the guys who'd tried to take us out had gone over the overpass in their SUV and died, it hadn't been hard to figure out who the hit had come from—the group behind the card counters we'd taken out a couple weeks earlier. Our team arrived at the crash just before the cops did, managed to pull one guy out of the wreck, and grabbed his wallet. With sirens on the way, they got the hell out of there.

Things were getting ugly, as they always did before they settled back down, so we increased security at the house as well as the office.

But everything would be fine in a few weeks. It always was. In the meantime, I had to insist Echo not leave the house.

I turned over in bed and snuggled my girl. Leo was on the other side but had somehow managed to hog more than half the bed.

Typical Leo.

I felt the bed move, as if someone had kicked it. Damn that brother of mine. He was going to keep me up all night long.

The bed moved again. "Leo, chill out."

When it happened a third time, I pushed back the covers with the intention of sending my brother back to his own bed.

But Leo hadn't been shaking the bed.

"What the—"

Echo opened her eyes and screamed.

Leo jumped out of bed.

"What the fuck are you doing here?" he yelled. "And how did you get in? Where is Smitt?"

Sal stood at the end of the bed, his smile slowly growing, and rubbing his hand on the pistol tucked into the front of his pants to let us know it was there. I knew that move. He'd taught it to me after my dad had disappeared.

While Leo pulled his pants on, Echo bolted up, holding the covers to her chin, the expression on her face rotating amid surprise, anger, and abject terror. I held my hands where Sal could see them, another thing he'd taught us, and got out of bed very slowly.

"Calm down, everyone. Keep your shit together," Sal said.

He stroked his gun again. "Don't worry about Smitt. I took care of him."

"What the hell does that mean?" I pulled my boxers on and reached for my trousers.

"I told you guys to get rid of the girl," he said.

Echo looked at us in horror. "Me? Get rid of me? What did I do?"

Sal shook his head, ignoring her questions. "I can see you made no progress in this area, even though I instructed you to right after you brought her home."

"Sal, can we step outside and talk about this? It really has nothing to do with Echo—"

"Shut. The. Fuck. Up. I've given you all the chances you needed, and more talking is not going to change things."

Had he lost his mind? To barge into our house in the middle of the night and scare the shit out of Echo? Jesus Christ. And where the fuck was Smitt?

I held my hands up in an attempt to reason. "Look, Sal. I think we just need to sit and have a talk. Let's go down to the library, and we'll open that nice bottle of scotch you gave us last Christmas."

I looked over at Echo. "You stay in bed. We'll take care of things."

To say Sal laughed at that was an understatement. He *boomed*. He always *boomed*. It was one of the things people loved about him.

And this time it was no different. Except that he had a gun, the rest of us were in various states of undress, and we weren't exactly feeling any affection for him.

I picked up Echo's robe from the floor and tossed it to her. She started putting it on underneath the covers while I pulled my jeans on.

"The girl will not be staying in bed." Sal gestured at her. "Get up. Now."

Again, Echo looked at Leo and me.

She burrowed deeper under the covers, as if they would protect her. "Uh... wh... why? I didn't do anything. What's going on here? What are you t... talking about?" she stuttered.

"C'mon," Sal repeated. "You're coming with me."

"Look, mister," Echo said suddenly, her eyes widening. "They did tell me to hit the road. But I came back. So it's really my fault. Don't get mad at them."

Where did she learn to act like that?

"Let me get dressed. I'll get the hell out of here. You'll never see me again, and neither will these guys."

I moved toward Sal, which only resulted in his pulling out his gun and pointing it at me, while his gaze remained on Echo.

Was he accepting her offer?

Apparently not.

He turned back to Leo and me. "Are you boys going to let a girl do your speaking for you? Or are you going to man up and accept that you broke the family rules?"

Leo took a step toward Sal. "No one broke any rules."

"Back up!" Sal barked.

"I know you wanted us to get rid of Echo," I said, "but I couldn't. I love her."

I glanced at Echo and saw her mouth drop open.

Sal burst out laughing, again. To think I loved this man like a father. And respected him.

"You're thinking with your little head, kid. You don't love this woman. You don't even know her. She was a goddamn cocktail waitress."

"Hey—" Echo started.

But Sal turned the gun on her. "Shut up."

"Fuck off, Sal," Leo said. "We've been together too long for something like this to go on."

"You," Sal said, gesturing at Echo, "c'mon. We're leaving."

She looked around frantically. "Can I get dressed? It will take me just a moment."

Sal rolled his eyes. "Go get your clothes and lay them out on the bed. Then you'll get dressed right here in front of all of us so there's no game playing."

Echo did as she was told and turned her back on Sal while she dressed. To his credit, he looked away.

She reached for her purse, which I'd seen her slip her phone into.

"I'm ready. Let's go." She held her head up bravely, but I knew she was trembling by the way she gripped her bag.

She headed for the door with Sal on her tail. But before he left, he turned back to us.

"You two stay here until you hear the front door slam. And if you fuck up, your pretty little friend here will pay the price."

At that moment, I would have liked to kill him with my bare hands. But I knew I needed to be patient. As he and Echo hustled down the stairs and across the foyer, I closed my eyes until the front door slammed.

I didn't just *want* to kill him. I was actually *going* to.

A car out in front of the house started and hit the road with a squeal.

"Let's find Smitt," Leo said, hitting my arm to snap me into action.

"Yeah."

Fuck. The last thing I wanted was for any harm to come to Echo. Maybe I'd been naïve to think I'd saved her from Loaded Dice, but now it was looking like I hadn't really done her any favors.

One good thing did come of Sal's invasion—I'd realized I loved her. I'd even said it out loud. I didn't know who'd been more surprised—Echo, or me.

Leo and I searched the house, yelling, "Smitt," until we heard banging coming from the library closet.

"Smitt, what the fuck?" Leo and I dragged him out of the closet. We untied his gag, as well as the ropes binding his hands.

"What happened?" I asked.

He rubbed a growing bump on the back of his head. "I heard an intruder. Somehow he got into the house. He must have sneaked up behind me and hit me, because I don't really remember anything more."

"You guys," Leo said, running in from the kitchen, "the side door was open with a house key in the lock."

I looked around the kitchen, and a sick thought crossed my mind.

Did Mary have something to do with this?

I knew she didn't like all the time Leo and I were spending with Echo. But I'd never imagined she was crazy enough to want to hurt her—or any of us, for that matter.

CHAPTER 43

ECHO

AND TO THINK things had been going so well.

Not.

First was the shootout at Loaded Dice. Then, I get followed to a shopping mall. Later, I go out for drinks with my best friend, and I come home to a spanking. My birthday night was highlighted by an assassination attempt, followed by being pulled out of bed by a psycho in the middle of the night. Screw Dini's advice —I should have just gone back to the shithole town I'd come from when I still had the chance. There, at least, my life wouldn't be in danger on a regular basis. I was in over my goddamn head with Vegas and these guys, and it looked like it might just cost me my life.

With the way things were going, it seemed like the

chances of ever getting back to my nasty little hometown were getting smaller and smaller.

It had taken me a minute to realize that the man who'd so rudely interrupted our sleep was the longtime associate and mentor to Luca and Leo, Sal Matteo. They'd told me how he more or less scooped them up and made them partners in his business when their dad went missing. How he was like a second father to them.

And now he was pointing a fucking gun at them?

What was wrong with these people?

If your relationships were so fragile and insignificant that you threatened people's lives the first time they pissed you off, well, I'd hate to see how they treated enemies.

Actually, I *had* seen how they treated enemies. I'd fallen flat on top of one of them the day the Borronis had 'saved' me at Loaded Dice.

I'd thought I was so resourceful when I'd arrived in Vegas, having found a place to live—however modest—and a job—however crappy. I had a roommate, a routine, and a life.

What more did a girl need? I was, for the most part, satisfied. I didn't ask for much, because I didn't need much. Things were perking along just fine.

Until the Borronis entered my life and fucked it all up.

Look at me now, I wanted to scream. Probably going to be six feet under in the very near future, all because I got mixed up with the wrong people.

Like my gran used to say, *a person is known by the company she keeps.*

She'd told me this when I started hanging out with school-skipping, pot-smoking kids in tenth grade. I was so ashamed of disappointing her that I sequestered myself in my bedroom and buried my nose in romance and mystery novels for the rest of the school year.

So why did I think it would be any different now? History repeats, and all that…

Make a bad decision once, and just keep on making them, should be my motto.

"Sal, where are you taking me?" I asked, forcing my voice to remain calm. Friendly, even. I was going to kill him with kindness, unless he killed me first.

It wasn't like I was an expert in being kidnapped, but since this was the second time in a month, I was getting the hang of it.

Stay calm. Make them believe you're on their side.

But don't take any shit.

He didn't answer my question.

"Doesn't seem like you have much respect for women, Sal. You won't answer my questions. Hell, you won't even look at me."

That got him.

He slammed his hand on the steering wheel. "You know, it's women like you—"

"What?" I interrupted in a raised voice. "*Women like me?* What the hell do you know about me? I was minding my own business when your *people* decided to kill everyone at the bar where I worked. Then your *people* decided I had to come home with them. Do you think this is what I want? That this is how I want to live?"

I crossed my arms and looked out the passenger window, mumbling about the unfairness of it all.

Yeah, I was putting on a show. But I had to get this cretin to see me in a different light.

"I'm taking you to a safe place. Then we'll decide what to do with you," he finally said.

Progress. The man was talking to me.

"Why don't you take me to the bus station? I'll hit the road. I've been wanting to get back to my sister in West Virginia, anyway."

Sal pulled into a parking garage, and a big metal door closed behind us. I was screwed.

He got out of the car and came around to the passenger side. When I didn't budge, he pulled my door open and yanked me out by the arm.

What the hell? Did he think I was going to make it easy for him?

"Hey!" I said, trying to sound tough.

But the truth was, I was scared shitless. Who knew what he had in store for me? I suspected it didn't include living in a cushy modern mansion and being given nice clothes and jewels on a regular basis.

Then a horrible thought occurred to me. While I was pretty sure he had no plans to offer me what Luca and Leo had, I sure hoped he didn't have anything sexual in mind. That's where I'd start to fight.

I'd better save my energy. Remain alert.

Sal pulled me into an elevator that took us from the garage up several floors. The doors opened into a dingy space with the feel of an unfinished attic's exposed beams and rough, wood floor. It was empty save for a rickety old table and chair and one light hanging overhead.

I stood in the middle of the room clutching my purse, when Sal opened the door to a smaller room and gestured that I enter. Inside, there was a shitty little mattress on the floor, and that was it.

I turned to look at Sal. "Is this where you're putting me? C'mon, let me stay in the larger room. I'm not going anywhere."

Without a word, he pulled the door shut. A key twisted and clicked, and I heard him get in the elevator and leave.

Well, shit.

I sat down on the dusty mattress, continuing to wonder how the hell I'd ended up with the shit end of the stick. Again.

I mean, doesn't the universe at some point decide you've had more than your share and send a few lucky breaks your way? You know, give the shit to someone else whose turn it was?

I texted Luca. Sal either hadn't thought I'd bring my

phone along, or he didn't think it would do me any good if I did.

I had no idea where I was and wasn't sure the guys would, either, so he was probably right on that count.

I sent a text to Luca.

i'm locked in a room and don't know where I am. but I'm fine. so far

His response came back immediately.

pretty sure we know where you are. stay put and keep quiet

Keep quiet? What the hell?

we'll be there soon

ok

What was the point of whisking me away if the guys could find me so easily? Seriously. These men needed to sharpen their skills.

I briefly considered texting Dini and Yasmina, just in case Luca and Leo didn't find me, and my life was cut short. But I thought that might be jumping the gun.

I put my phone away to preserve the battery and lay back on the mattress. To occupy my thoughts, I imagined how I might fix up the room if it were mine. Kind of like how someone had fixed up my room at the guys' house.

And I slowly drifted to sleep.

CHAPTER 44

ECHO

I woke up with a start, thanks to a terrible nightmare. In it, Sal was going to 'give' me away to another of his henchmen as a gift. I'd never see anyone I knew or loved again, and I was vacillating between sheer horror and abject sadness that my life was essentially over.

That's when I heard some sort of commotion outside my room. I pressed my ear against the door and heard Luca and Leo. And, of course, Sal.

Ohthankgod.

But how fucking lame was it that Sal couldn't even find a place to hide me where the Borronis couldn't find me?

Or, maybe it was that he never thought they'd defy him and come after me.

Naïve man. I mean, Luca had just said he fucking loved me.

Luca *loved* me. Holy crap.

"If you boys want to live to see your next birthdays, you'll turn around and get the hell out of here," I heard Sal say.

"Look, Sal," Luca said, "I have an idea of what your plan is for Echo, and I want to offer to buy her from you. We'll settle things right now and forget this ever happened."

Sal burst out laughing. I could just picture him dropping his bald head back, his wrinkles accentuated by the motion in his face.

"You know, I've loved you boys like you were my own. For how many years now have we been a team? A family? And now we're down to this."

"It doesn't have to be like this, Sal," Luca said.

"Oh, but it does. You see, Echo is mine now."

Huh?

I wasn't being given to a henchman as a gift like I'd dreamed?

"What are you saying?" Luca asked.

"She's mine. And she will be mine until I say otherwise. She should have been mine since the beginning. Not yours, or your brother's. I saw her at the club, too, and I wanted her before you sank your claws in her."

Wait. What?

"I'm taking her for myself. You boys will just have to

get over it. Go find some other bitch to fuck. There are plenty of them out there. I want this one."

That's what this was all about? I sure didn't see that coming. And I didn't think Luca or Leo did, either.

"Sal, that's not going to happen," Luca said. "You've been good to us, but our relationship is over now."

Holy fuck.

A gunshot rang out and I heard groaning. I ran back to my mattress in the corner and cowered, unsure about whether a bullet could come through the flimsy wall, or who might be hurt and who might not.

I realized that if anything happened to Luca or Leo, my heart would be broken. Plain and simple. They'd tried to take good care of me, god knew. But there was danger at every turn that not even they could protect me from.

They should never have brought me into their lives. It had been just as dangerous for them as it had been for me.

Just as I was sinking into some serious depths of despair, the door to my room crashed opened.

I squeezed my eyes shut and held my breath. I didn't know who it would be and whether they'd have a bullet for me, too.

"It's safe. You can come out."

I opened my eyes to Leo's grim smile. My heart thumped. Who'd been shot?

Luca or Sal?

I was going to be sick.

Pushing myself to my feet, I walked to the doorway on shaking legs and gripped the doorjamb while I peered around the corner.

Leo nodded at me.

Across the room, Sal was sprawled on the floor in a spreading pool of blood.

Both pity and revulsion washed over me at the same time. I was sorry for the old man, but he'd got what he had coming.

With tears in his eyes, Luca took Sal's hand. "I'm sorry it had to end like this Sal. I loved you like a father."

Sal lifted his head an inch or two. "I want to tell you something before I go," he rasped.

Luca leaned his ear closer.

Sal sputtered and coughed.

"I killed your mother."

Oh my god.

The words hit Luca like a truck, both literally and figuratively, as he dropped Sal's hand with a *thud* and backed away in horror. Both he and Leo paled, their betrayal one of the saddest fucking things I'd ever seen.

Luca shook his head in confusion.

"What, Sal? You killed our *mother*?" Luca asked, incredulous.

"I… I'm sorry. I'm so sorry. We were… a thing. But in those days it had to stay quiet. Your mom threatened to make our affair public… I had no choice…"

"Holy fucking shit," Luca whispered. "And as if that

was not enough, you wanted to take Echo from us, too?"

Sal laid his head back down and closed his eyes. All he could do was nod.

He was going to be gone soon. He knew it and we knew it.

"What the fuck is wrong with you? What kind of man are you?" Luca quietly asked.

"You deserve to die alone like the dog that you are," Leo said, pulling Luca and me toward the elevator.

Before we got on, I turned to see Sal's hand reaching toward us. I wasn't sure if it was for help or redemption, but I knew there'd be neither.

"Go to hell, you fucker," I said as the elevator doors closed.

CHAPTER 45

LUCA

FIVE MONTHS LATER

After Sal's death, Leo and I began to divest ourselves of several of our businesses, including the casinos. Knowing they were built by someone like Sal had changed our commitment to them. They were suddenly unsavory. Actually worse than unsavory. We weren't in the most respected of professions by a long shot, but there was honor among thieves.

So to speak.

And knowing he was behind our mother's death—well, that was unfathomable. We were still shaken by that revelation and probably always would be. Irrevocably. As much as it hurt, he'd done us a favor with his deathbed confession. I would have hated to revere the man in death, never knowing what he was really made of.

Did he have something to do with our father's disappearance so many years ago? We'd never know.

But we had our suspicions.

Our poor mother, having taken up with that bastard. It hurt to hear that, almost more than I could bear. It was going to take a long time to come to terms with it.

But there were good things going on to take it off my mind.

I drove up to the diner Echo had opened just the week before. Our smart girl had managed to pull off a smash hit opening, hard for any restaurant in Vegas, let alone an old-school diner boasting signature *pie*. I'd had my doubts when she'd shared her vision about whether the Vegas crowd would be down with such a quaint and homey concept, but it turned out to be just what people were hankering for.

A return to the past. Comfort food. Happy memories.

There'd been lines out the door since opening, and Echo was working day and night. Once she had the kinks worked out and could slow down a bit, I'd talk her into hiring a manager. But as it stood right now, she wanted to run the show. I didn't blame her. The diner was her baby.

And her sister was arriving tomorrow.

I pulled into the overflow parking lot and waved at Smitt, who was bringing the diner's security team up to speed.

Did a diner really need security? Most probably did not. But this wasn't any old kind of diner, and Vegas wasn't any old kind of city. It could be glamorous, and it could be rough-and-tumble. Best to be prepared for anything.

Besides, I wouldn't let Echo go anywhere without security, anyway. I wasn't fucking crazy. There were other Sals in the world, and it was my job to keep her safe from them.

I looked up at the diner's bright neon sign. Its name made me smile.

DIRTY GAME

I walked into the bustling place, waiting to catch Echo's gaze. She had a phone to her ear and was talking to a customer at the same time. I'd told her what she was doing was too much work for one person, but she wasn't ready to listen to me. Yet.

When she finally looked my way, I pointed at my watch. Enough of the diner—it was *my* time—Game time—and nothing was infringing on that.

"Hey, handsome," she said, planting a juicy kiss on my lips. "Let's get out of here before someone else stops me."

I took a discreet handful of her ass and squeezed. "Yeah. Let's make a break for it."

She looked at me and laughing, grabbed my hand, and we ran all the way to my car.

"Cripes. I'm tired. But we sold out of pie again." She leaned on the headrest and turned to smile at me as I pulled into traffic.

"Wow. That's fucking amazing. Is the pastry chef able to keep up with the orders?"

"She's gonna have to bring in one or two more people to help. Thank god we built out that big freaking kitchen. I'd thought it was too ambitious, but what a stroke of luck that you insisted."

I reached for her hand. "I know a few things about business."

It felt good to be involved in something outside the 'family' business, and especially one that was off to a roaring start. Of course, I couldn't take credit for that. The vision and execution were really all Echo's. She'd been smart enough to ask the right questions to set herself up for success, and her instincts were mind-blowing. I'd never seen anything like it. She took to running a restaurant like it was second nature.

And what was even cooler was that all the top chefs in Vegas were making a point to come by and try the place out. In a city where fine dining was an art form, people were eager to try something in a more down-home setting.

As for myself, if I didn't stop eating the leftover pie Echo kept bringing home, I'd have to go shopping for bigger pants.

"What are we doing for dinner?" she asked.

"Leo's cooking."

Her head snapped in my direction. "Again?"

Since we'd fired Mary for helping Sal break into our house and given her a one-way ticket out of town, Leo had been experimenting in the kitchen. Some of his dishes were bloopers, and some were pretty damn edible.

That night, he knocked it out of the park. His filet mignon with pepper sauce and roasted vegetables were at least as good as anything Mary ever made.

"Thank you, Leo, that was an amazing dinner," Echo said, finishing before me like she often did.

Fucking hot. A woman who loved her food.

"Yeah. That kicked ass," I added.

"So what's on the agenda for tonight?" Echo asked. "Is The Game on?"

If Echo wanted to play The Game, we played it. No questions asked. And I could tell from the twinkle in her eye that our girl was ready to have some fun.

We headed to the library for some after-dinner drinks. Well, seltzer water for me.

"I've got a gift for you," Leo said after we'd settled in.

Echo wasn't the only one surprised by Leo's

announcement. He wasn't one to give gifts, especially when he was the secondary in The Game. But it was all good.

He pulled a small velvet box out of his pants pocket and presented it to Echo.

She looked between the two of us as she opened it, and gasped. "Oh my god, it's stunning." She pulled a ring out of the box and slipped it on.

Leo smiled proudly. "It's a double ring so you always remember Luca and me, and The Game."

Echo tilted her head. "Remember? Is there something going on that I don't know about?" she asked, looking between us.

Leo crossed the room to give Echo a kiss on her temple. "The Game is over."

"Huh?" Echo asked. "What? Why?"

She did not look happy.

I took her hand. "Yeah, baby, The Game is over. We're not playing it anymore."

She scowled. "Why *not*?"

Leo laughed. "Relax. Nothing is wrong. It's just time for you and Luca to explore… what you have. I'm bowing out so you can do that."

Echo's mouth opened, then slowly closed. She jumped up and threw her arms around my brother.

"Oh, Leo. You are a very special man." She pulled back to look at him, tears in her eyes.

"And you, my dear, are a very special woman," he said.

He turned to me with a smile. "She's all yours, bro. Treat her well."

It was Leo's idea to step aside. He'd seen what was growing between Echo and me, and the last thing he wanted was for our kinky little game to get in the way.

The Game had been fun. A lot of fun. But it had served its purpose. We'd enjoyed it but never expected it to last forever.

"Thanks, bro," I said.

He saluted us and left the library.

I pulled Echo closer.

"Did you know he was going to do that?" she asked.

I nodded. "He discussed it with me first. Are you okay with it?"

Christ, I hoped she was okay with it.

"I am. The Game has been awesome, but I agree, it's time for it to end."

"You're not sorry?" I asked.

"Nope. Ending The Game means a new beginning."

I ran my hand through her long dark hair. I knew she'd get it.

"Remember when you told Sal you loved me, during his little home invasion?" she asked.

Of course I remembered. I'd wondered if she remembered it, because it had never come up again.

I nodded.

"Well, I never had the chance to respond to you because, you know, Sal was kidnapping me and stuff. I was a little distracted," she said, rolling her eyes.

What a fucked-up night that was.

"But I think you already knew my feelings. Even though I didn't say them out loud."

I was dying to tear her clothes off but forced myself to sit still and listen. "Is there something stopping you from saying them now?"

She faced me head-on. "Luca Borroni. Even though you supposedly 'saved' me from the carnage at Loaded Dice, forced me to come live with you, almost got me killed in a drive-by shooting, and had a crazy boss who tried to kidnap me to make me his own, I'm still here."

I rolled my eyes. "That's big of you, Echo Duncan. I appreciate it."

"Oh wait, I forgot Mary, the crazy cook. Anyway, you're welcome. Most women would have hightailed it the hell out of here by now."

Fair enough.

"So why didn't you split?" I ask.

She looked down at her fidgeting hands. "Because I love you, too."

There.

Looking back up at me, she leaned toward my ear. "We're now going to play something called the un-game," she whispered.

"Un-game. What the hell is that?"

"It's a game with rules we make up as we go, where no one wins and no one loses."

Sounded like a fucking winner to me.

Did you like *Dirty Game*? Learn about the next book in Dark Mafia Games,
Nasty Bet

I hope you loved reading this book as much as I loved writing it. Please visit my store to learn more about my books, and to buy directly from me! https://mikalaneshop.com/

FREE BONUS EPILOGUE
Check it out here!

Dear Reader:

I'm USA TODAY bestselling romance author Mika Lane, and am OBSESSED with bringing you sassy, steamy stories with imperfect heroines and the bad-a*s dudes they bring to their knees. I'll always bring you my signature humor and heat, topped off with a modern-day happily ever after.

My first book ever was *The Day I Ate the Milkyway,* a true fourth-grade masterpiece illustrated with crayons and bound with construction paper and glue. Nowadays, steamy romance gives purpose to my days and nights as I create worlds and characters that tickle the imagination. I live in magical Northern California with my own handsome alpha dude, sometimes known as Mr. Mika Lane, and two devilish cats named Chuck and Murray.

A dual citizen of the United States and Ireland, I have on more than one occasion spent my last dollar on a plane ticket somewhere, and am always planning my next escape. I often try new recipes on unsuspecting friends, search out hiding places to read undisturbed, and sadly kill every houseplant I bring home.

I LOVE to hear from readers when I'm not dreaming up naughty tales to share. Visit my online shop https://mikalaneshop.com/ and say hello https://mikalaneshop.com/pages/meet-mika.

xoxo, Mika